QUEEN ANNE'S CURSE

First edition. January 28, 2024.

Copyright © 2024 Stephen C. Challis.

ISBN: 979-8989961917

Written by Stephen C. Challis.

I0451685

Dedication

Queen Anne's Curse

Revised edition 01/2024

Stephen Challis

The author and editor wrote and edited this book in Microsoft Word, using United Kingdom English.

Dedication

This book is dedicated to the unknown archer whose remains were recovered from a storeroom in the wreck of the Carrick Warship, Mary Rose, by divers from The Mary Rose Trust, and to the rest of the crew who perished with him on 19th July, 1545.
May they rest in peace.

Forward

John Rombaud was a troubled man. He had recently returned from England to English occupied Calais after his latest and most notable execution. The year was 1536 and his latest victim had been the consort of the English Monarch Henry Tudor. Henry the VIII as history would record him. Queen Anne Boleyn had paid the price for her indiscretions in court. She had faced death with dignity, and a courage beyond that of her 34 years. Rombaud was a professional. If he had any pity or concern for his victim, it did not show.

The well-placed blow instantly severed her head, and the loose fitting blindfold had come loose as it struck the floor. Her eyes flickered open and seemed to focus on her killer before her head rolled away, coming to rest in the straw on the scaffold. Blood from the severed jugular continued to pump from the torso while most of the small crowd watched in sombre respect; there was no cheering.

The vision would haunt his dreams for many years. He did not know this woman, only her status. In the power struggles of 17th century England, it seemed unlikely that she had committed any of the crimes she had been accused of, but he was not concerned about that. He received a generous payment for his work, and the queen's distraught ladies-in-waiting swiftly covered the bloody body and severed head.

Henry did not attend the execution, but he gave strict instructions for disposing of the body without ceremony, in a private chapel. One of the tearful ladies-in-waiting had approached him and thanked him for doing his duty swiftly, and without causing suffering. As she bent forward, she clasped his hand; startled, he looked down at the gold and Emerald encrusted ring pressed into his palm. She whispered softly;

"Good sir, this is my ladi's ring. It has brought her nothing but pain and suffering in this world. Please take it far from this land, ensure it does not bring misfortune to any other woman. My Lady cursed it in our presence and all who would wear it."

Then she was gone, back to the body, in tears.

Now, back at his home in France, Rombaud stared at the ring. He knew it was valuable, no doubt, worth a king's ransom. He chuckled at the irony, but he was also aware he could hardly sell it. Henry had decreed that all portraits of the late queen be destroyed. Her name and memory were to be stricken from public record. Should he find out that Anne's personal gift from him had been stolen by a lady-in-waiting, and given to her executioner, his rage would be indeterminable. So he needed to dispose of it, discreetly, and preferably swiftly.

Until then, the ring must disappear. Of course, the obvious thought occurred to him he should just destroy it. He seriously considered doing just that for several days. But the ring was exquisite, a gift from one of the most powerful rulers in the world to his wife. In this day and age, people believed emeralds offered the wearer the protection of God, a powerful image. Of course, Rombaud had no such beliefs. The demise of its former owner testified to the shallowness of such claims, yet still he could not see his way to destroy it. The following morning, he set off for Loire Valley. There, he maintained a summer residence, obtained some years before, in payment for a job that was, shall we say, not strictly legal. There, he had placed the ring in a lead box, and sealed it inside with a hot iron, before burying it adjacent to an outside privy: a place where no man would tarry longer than he had to. And there it may have remained for all time, save an incident in the life of Rombaud that resurrected it, and set it on a course that would change many lives forever.

Six years later, with no sign of interest from England, or its monarch, regarding the ring, the master swordsman and executioner had moved on, no longer taking commissions for legalised murder, he was earning a good living as a sword maker, and instructor. He had married, and the unpleasant memories of Queen Anne Boleyn had faded from his daily thoughts. His country retreat in the Loire Valley was becoming a very much under-used facility. His wife had been urging him to sell it and use the capital to expand the sword academy. It was a sound plan, but then there was the ring. It is highly unlikely that anyone would ever find it. However, if a new owner discovers it and attempts to sell it, someone might identify its unique design. And as the previous owner, the trail would lead back to him. Quite simply, it was a chance he could not take. His wife, though aware of his previous occupation, and even the fact he had wielded the sword that dispatched King Henry's second wife, still did not know of the ring, and he intended to keep it that way.

On his next visit, he would retrieve it and dispose of it in the jewellery markets of Boulogne.

That did not happen. Relations between England and France had deteriorated over France's support for the Scots, and the English who already occupied Calais marched on, and then lay siege to Boulogne.

Having safely recovered the ring, he once again considered destroying it. But aware of its significance and value, he again could not bring himself to take that last step. Despite it being sealed underground for 6 years, the ring was in remarkable condition. Set in gold, the 7 emeralds sparkled with a light of their own. Radiant and alluring, like a beautiful woman, but behind the façade lay the hint of a dark and malevolent heart. For three days he kept the ring hidden at his residence in St. Omer, but then disaster hit. His housemaid found it, and assuming it belonged to his wife, had handed it to her. This inevitably had led to a somewhat awkward conversation. Faced with little choice, he revealed to her the full story behind his possession of it. For a moment, she stared at the ring.

"And you say the Queen cursed the ring and all future owners?"

Rombaud nodded. *"Well, even if Henry has no interest in it, what woman would want to own it, let alone wear it?"*

His wife smiled.

"You know little of women, my love. I know of many who would love to own a royal ring, regardless of any curse. We have to find a buyer who is

not likely to betray us to the King. I know of such a man. Oh, he will haggle over the price, and I will allow him to cheat me a little, and he can sell it on for a good profit."

Rombaud was unsure.

"*How can you be sure he won't just inform the English?*"

His wife smiled and patted his hand.

"*The man I have in mind lost two sons to Henry's army in Ireland, fighting for the Earl of Kildare. He hates Henry Tudor, and all the English, for that matter.*"

Rombaud realised he was no longer in control. The plan seemed foolproof and the following day, Marie Rombaud travelled to Calais and visited the shop owned by a Monsignor Francis De Winter.

British born De Winter was a renowned jeweller and traded with many rich and aristocratic residents of both French and British descent. The sight of the ring intrigued De Winter immediately. Marie told him the story, but omitted her husband's name; just that he had received it from a man who had got it from a lady-in-waiting at the scene of the execution.

De Winter was a shrewd entrepreneur and knew the story was likely true. He had heard stories of a ring that seemed to have vanished after the queens' execution. Such a history would command a top price. After examining the ring, he handed it back to Marie.

"*Well, it is a fine ring, madam, and of course it may have come from England, but there is no proof it did so. And with the current situation between France and England, money is, of course, tight. However, to help you out, I can make you a fair offer of 20 testoons.*"

Marie knew the offer was woefully below the value, and decided to play a short round of haggling. Just enough to make the dealer worried he may lose the deal.

She replied,

"Well! Your offer is considerably lower than a friend of my husband, a Monsignor Rabat, who also deals in fine jewellery offered me. Do you know him?"

De Winter knew him well, and that he was a man of greater means than himself. He did not relish the thought of losing such a valuable piece to him. He thought for a moment before replying,

"Of course you could sell to Monsignor Rabat, but he is friendly to the British Governor here. There may be, shall we say, awkward questions. However, I want to give you a fair deal. So I may stretch to 25 testoons."

Marie waited for what seemed like ages before replying, putting on the most reluctant voice she could muster.

"If you make it 28 testoons, we have a deal."

De Winter could hardly believe his luck, 28 Testoons for a ring that could easily fetch 75 in the right market.

He extended his hand.

"I think we have a deal, madam."

Table of Chapter Contents

Epilogue

Bibliography & Acknowledgements

Chapter 1

Questions

David Spencer awoke suddenly. His breathing was rapid, and his heartbeat seemed abnormally fast. He glanced around the room. Slowly, it came into focus. It was just a dream, an intense dream which was now evaporating into the sunlight and the sense of reality that flooded into his world. What was it about? Did it involve some sort of warning questions he could not answer?

He looked to his left, where last night he had seen Debbie lying alongside him. Now there was an empty space, covers thrown back. A quick glance at the alarm clock showed the time: 7:47 AM. He lay there for a few minutes. It was Sunday. No work today, so why was Debbie up so early. The sounds of clinking dishes from the kitchen told him she was still in the house. He sat up and swung his legs over the side of the bed.

His heartbeat was now returning to normal, and the sweating had subsided. His first thought was to head for the shower, but hell, it was Sunday, and the shower could wait. He threw on his short dressing coat that barely covered his naked form and headed for the kitchen. *"Hi sweetheart, you're up early."*

Debbie turned to look at him directly and started to answer; instead, she smiled half-heartedly and asked if he fancied a coffee.

David smiled back. *"That sounds like a plan."*

Debbie took the coffee filter jar and began to fill it while David looked around for his cell phone. Finally, he gave up.

"Sweetheart, have you seen my phone?"

His wife looked up and momentarily, a look of almost guilt flashed over her face, before she replied.

"Yes, I picked it up this morning on the bedroom floor. I thought it was mine."

She took the phone from her robe pocket and handed it to him. He nodded and sat back down. As he turned on the phone, he failed to notice that it was set on contacts, but he quickly switched to messages and scanned through them.

Debbie looked calm and pretty cute in her skimpy baby doll and open robe, but inside, her mind was anything but calm. Finally, she looked up.

"So, how did you sleep?"

"Well, to be honest, I'm not sure. I woke up suddenly. I think I was having a nightmare, my heart was racing, and I felt pretty scared."

If he had been expecting sympathy, then he was to be disappointed.

"What was the dream about?" she said softly.

He looked up at her; she was not smiling, but had a determined look on her face, a look that all but demanded an answer.

"That's the weird thing I don't know. I cannot recall any details. Something about being trapped, being alone, and being terrified. It was surreal. I've had nightmares before, but I always remembered them, this time, nothing."

David's reply wrong footed her and left her with no opportunity to access his inner thoughts. She sipped her coffee before replying,

"I think you have had several dreams recently. I think something is troubling you."

David nodded.

"I've noticed that, but I can't imagine what it is. Work's OK. Our relationship seems pretty good, and we do not seem to have any money problems. What do you think?"

Debbie shrugged

"Beats me, sweetie, but it is a worry. Maybe you should speak to your doctor."

David laughed.

"I'm sure the inspector would love that. The force shrink would have a field day."

Of course, Debbie knew that only too well. Both were serving police officers in the Hampshire Constabulary and had been married in 1998 almost 3 years ago. So far, the force had assigned both of them to the western area, and they were serving at Portsmouth and Portswood stations on corresponding shifts. However, that accommodation was not a forgone conclusion. It was not unknown for couples out of favour with the hierarchy to separate them to encourage resignation. The golden rule was not to rock the boat, and keep private matters private.

There the matter rested, but David knew it would not go away. The events of that night proved him right.

David got in at 10:30 PM after his day shift. Debbie was on split shift, and would be off at midnight. After changing and pouring himself a Rum and Coke cocktail, he settled down to await her.

It had been a pretty rough shift, and the local news was showing a repeat of the salvage operation of a Tudor warship in the Solent, called the 'Mary Rose'. They had recovered it in 1982 the year he had been born. David had never been that interested in history; and although the operation had been the talk of the region at the time, he thought it was all ancient history. Nothing connected with his real passion, supporting the Saints, Southampton's premier football club. He quickly began to doze.

At a quarter after midnight, Debbie pulled into the drive. Noticing that the ground floor light was on, she picked up the pizza from the passenger seat and entered the house. The disturbance awoke David, who immediately began coughing and choking. As Debbie reached him, he was already on his knees. He reached out and grabbed her hands tightly and painfully, almost as if his life depended on it. She struggled free and yelled his name. The effect was instantaneous. He opened his eyes and looked wildly around.

"Thank God," he murmured before embracing her. Debbie could feel the sweat moistening his t-shirt and felt his pounding heart. This was not the first nightmare her husband had experienced. Sometimes he called out a woman's name, other times he swore, before waking. Debbie still did not know what was troubling him, but was beginning to suspect it was nothing to do with any other woman. This was something far deeper and scarier. They both sat up late talking, in part, because David did not want to return to sleeping, for fear of what awaited him in the subconscious area of his mind. As for Debbie, she knew she needed to do something. When she really needed advice, the one person she could always count on was her father. A retired police Chief Inspector with 25 years' service. He earned great respect and held various achievements, including being the Master of the local Masonic Lodge. This position allowed him to connect with professionals from different fields, such as doctors and individuals with academic backgrounds. That morning, she called him.

....

Two days later, Retired Police Chief Inspector Geoffrey Hawthorne arrived at the Spencer's. David was not home, so his daughter requested this meeting to be arranged for that time. Hawthorne greeted her warmly, with a hug and kiss on the forehead. But he sensed right away that this was no normal social visit. Debbie was nervous, and at least to a trained police officer, it was obvious. She made two mugs of coffee and sat down. There was a moment's awkward silence, which her father broke.

"Ok Kitten, so what's the problem?"
Debbie tried to smile reassuringly, which failed. Then she relaxed.

"Well, it's David."

Her father smiled and patted her hand gently.

"I guessed as much."

He said gently.

"So what's he done?"

Debbie looked down, as if avoiding her father's face.

"That's just it. He has done nothing at all. He's his normal self during the day, but recently he has had awful nightmares. He wakes up shaking and sweating. Sometimes he calls out a name, but he can never remember what he was dreaming about. But one thing is certain; he's scared, very scared when he wakes up. I suppose he should see a doctor, but you know the consequences of that. The force medical officer would have to put in a report, and, well, bang goes his career."

Hawthorne looked at his daughter. Like most parents, he could not look at her without seeing the little 5 to 7-year-old full of wonder and questions; such as, why is the sky blue, and what makes the sun shine. But now he sensed she really needed to hear advice that he felt unable to give. However, he knew his daughter had made the right choice in seeking his advice.

"I see. So what do you think is behind this work stress or something else?"

"I thought of work stress. I know soldiers can suffer from PTSD after intense combat experience, and possibly police officers as well. But David is not in that category. He's just a normal DC, dealing with frauds and burglaries. Nothing that would explain this.

When he began calling out a woman's name, 'Joan', in his dreams, I considered he was having an affair. And even checked his phone for contacts named Joan, but there was nothing there. But he doesn't act in any way guilty. Last Monday he dozed off in front of the telly and woke up choking and gasping for air. He grabbed hold of me as if I had saved his life. I thought at first he was dreaming about something scary he had seen on the telly, you know, a spooky show or something, but he said he did not watch too much that night, just some boring history show on the Mary Rose. You know how boring he finds history. No, really, Dad, I don't understand what is going on.

Hawthorne said nothing for a moment. He knew of cases where the pressures of police work could cause depression and anxiety. But this behaviour didn't seem to fit the bill. He liked David, and remembered when he had come round nervously to ask for Debbie's hand in marriage, an outdated gesture in 1988, but well received. He liked him then and still did. His daughter seemed blissfully happy until now.

"Well, I'm not sure if I can help personally, but I may know someone who may. Let me reassure you, he is not a police officer. He is actually a psychiatrist."

Debbie shook her head.

"David's not crazy dad, if word got out, then it's a medical discharge. We both know that."

Her father again took her hand.

"No one is suggesting David is crazy. Believe me, I've met several crazies, and I know the difference. But whatever is troubling him is locked in his mind. If we can unlock it, we may get an insight into the cause."

Debbie seemed to relax a little. So he continued.

"Now I cannot promise anything until I can speak to him. Quite frankly, I'm a little out of my depth kitten, but the man I'm thinking of specialises in this stuff. I'll call him and get back to you. Until then, be there for him when he needs it, when he has another episode."

Hawthorne left the house, a troubled man. He knew he had to help, but was unsure of how. He decided the best place to start was some background checks. Treat it like an investigation. Once back in the car, He took out his cell phone.

"Susan; It's Geoffrey. Can I come round this evening? I want to talk to you. It's about David."

....

After the pleasantries were dispensed with David's parents, Susan and Philip Spencer sat down, intrigued that Geoffrey had expressly asked them not to notify David or Debbie of his visit.

True to form, Geoffrey got straight to the point.

"Something's come up that concern Debbie and David that may have consequences for all of us. Before I go into it, I have a question. It may sound odd, but it may be a key to everything."

"When he was young, did David ever suffer from nightmares, particularly scary ones about choking or being smothered?"

Susan and her husband became quiet before Susan said,

"Drowning? It was drowning? How could you possibly know that?"

"I didn't know till now. You see, David has been experiencing recurring dreams lately, and it has led to Debbie confiding in me. I'm trying to uncover some facts involving no one connected to the force. So what can you tell me about these dreams?"

Susan looked up but saw nothing but concern in Geoffrey's eyes.

"It started when he was about 7. He woke up screaming and thrashing about almost as if he was swimming. At first we thought it was because he had started swimming lessons at school, but his PE instructor said he was a very willing pupil and was learning fast. He was excited about learning to swim. Anyway, the dreams continued intermittently, and thank god he finally grew out of them."

"Did he ever remember the dreams, details, and such?"

Susan's husband chipped in.

"Well, nothing that made too much sense. He said he was sinking, and they were crazy and stupid, but no names. I remember on one occasion he spoke of the frogs, they were killing him. As I said, stupid small boy stuff. All kids have them. When I was small, I was afraid of birds, imagined one was going to eat me. That was probably because of my parents allowing me to watch the Hitchcock film The Birds on TV in the early 60s. But Frogs, that was just loopy."

The remark was made to sound lighthearted, but it did nothing to change the mood.

Susan spoke next, and her question was straight to the point.

"Are you suggesting that David has a mental problem or illness?"

Geoffrey shook his head.

"No, I am not. But something is troubling him. I'm just trying to find out what it is, and if I, and in fact all of us, may be able to help. One other thing, did David ever mention the name Joan in his dreams?"

Susan thought for a moment.

"Actually, he did, well, sort of; he was restless one night. When he was about 6, I touched his hand and without opening his eyes he whispered,"

"Fair Joan"

"I remember thinking it was a phrase he must have seen on TV. He was, well, into knights and damsels in distress at the time. Anyway, he calmed down, and I didn't wake him. Strange, though, that you should mention that name."

Her husband chipped in

"Is the name important?"

Geoffrey smiled

"Probably not, but unfortunately I tend to fall back on my police background when trying to solve mysteries. In a criminal investigation, even the slightest fact can crack a case. David's problem, whatever it is, is influencing their marriage, which concerns me. I don't think David will be able to help much, as he can never remember the dreams or details. It's a worry, but I think I know someone who may be able to help."

Chapter 2

Going back

One of the principle rules of Freemasonry; is that conversations in the lodge remain confidential. There are some restrictions on discussion topics, as any Mason will tell you, but the subject of family concerns was not among them. Geoffrey had spent an hour outlining his concerns about his son-in-law to fellow Mason Dr Andrew McMaster, an eminent psychiatrist in practice in Southampton, who lived in Portswood. Dr McMaster listened respectfully. Nodding occasionally as he thought fit.

"Well, Geoffrey, I am not sure if I am the right person to help. If David truly has no recollection of these dreams, and they are the only symptom of abnormality, I am tempted to say they may be psychosomatic, evidence of some underlying fear, even though that fear may be totally irrational. Let me try to explain. Several years ago, I spoke to a colleague of mine who had a patient with deep anxiety problems. He showed me a painting at his house of a tropical island being lashed by hurricane-force winds. He complimented her on the excellent execution of the painting. Her reply was unexpected. She said, 'No Doctor, you miss the point. This painting conveys what I felt like deep inside before you rescued me.' In that context, it became a very frightening painting. The human mind is extremely complex. It often puts up shutters to shield itself from unpleasant memories. Speaking to him in confidence may uncover that fear, but I may be able to offer advice. A colleague of mine, Dr Ruth Walters, this may be more her sort of field."

Geoffrey seemed surprised

"Another Psychiatrist?"

"No, she is a hypnotherapist, a specialist in this sort of thing. I can arrange an introduction if you wish."

"Hypnosis? That may be worth a try, assuming I can persuade him to try. If I can get my daughter to agree, that's half the battle."

Geoffrey decided that his next step was to speak to David and his daughter alone. The fact that both were in the Police Force and that he was a retired police officer should allay any fears David may have. Anyway, he reasoned, David was probably as eager to get to the root of this matter as Debbie was. He called her and set up a meeting at their home.

....

"Doctor Walters will see you now."

Geoffrey got up from the chair and entered the office. Ruth Walters was not at all what he expected. She was a slightly built woman in her early 30s with dark hair and a warm smile. Not the 50-year-old bespectacled battle-axe he had envisaged. Her office was modern and had the obligatory couch against the wall, a bookcase with medical books and a diploma in a case on the wall.

"Now, inspector, Dr McMaster tells me you have a perplexing case involving your son; specifically, disturbing and frightening dreams. What else can you tell me?"

Geoffrey related everything he had learned from his daughter, pausing whenever he noticed her making notes.

"What was your daughter's reaction when he called out the name Joan?"

Geoffrey was ready for that one.

"Well, obviously, she was suspicious, but I do not think it was significant. I spoke to his mother a while ago, who told me he used to call out the same name when he was 6 years old during nightmares. Of course, they were not so severe then, but it appears they have returned. I would like to know why, and I think hypnosis may hold the key."

Dr Walters said nothing at first. She seemed deep in thought, and then she replied.

"I can see why my colleague asked me to see you. Your son's case seems very unusual. I would need to see him, of course; I don't do diagnosis on hearsay, as I'm sure, and being a former police officer, you will appreciate. However, I will say that this case does somewhat intrigue me. If I can, I would like to help your son."

Reassured, Geoffrey thanked her and left; looking forward to his meeting that Saturday with his daughter and David. However, the meeting did not go well. David was unwilling to even consider meeting a shrink, as he called Dr Walters. When Debbie tried to change his mind, he became hostile to both his wife and Geoffrey.

As he left, David tried to ease the tension.

"Look Geoffrey, I know you mean well, and you have my health as your primary concern, but really, this is something I can work out. It's just stupid dreams. That's all."

Geoffrey had run into a brick wall. But that night, things took a turn for the worst.

Around 3:00 AM, David began convulsing and thrashing wildly. Immediately, Debbie sat up in bed, and reached for him. David's blow struck her just above his chin, knocking her violently out of bed. Her scream woke him. As he returned to consciousness, he saw Debbie in a crumpled heap on the floor. He moved towards her and she yelled at him to stay away from her. He watched, mortified, as she headed for the bathroom and applied a cold water soaked sponge to her cheek.

For almost twenty minutes she did not speak, as David tried desperately to explain he did not know what he was doing, and that he had been asleep. Of course, Debbie knew that was probably true, but she also knew that she could not continue to trust him to share her bed.

"David, you know I love you, but we just cannot keep ignoring this. You have a problem; this Dr Walters may be able to help. So, I'm sorry, unless you agree to see her, we seriously need to discuss a separation."

David had no choice. He had let the situation continue, but now it threatened his marriage, and that was unacceptable. After a moment, his voice softened.

"OK Debbie, of course you are right, I will see this woman shrink, but I will need some convincing that she can help."

Debbie said nothing, but moved her things into the spare room. David did not object. He knew that the bond of trust had been broken, and he was aware that he would need to put in a lot of effort to restore it.

....

Three days later, David arrived at the office of Doctor Walters. Debbie had driven him there and had decided not to stay. Instead, she joined her father at a small café just off the high street. At a recent development called Gun wharf Quays.

David entered the office and signed in; he glanced cursorily at two other patients. Both seemed young. And one looked vaguely familiar; he was making an appointment at the reception desk, and left before David could place him. The other patient wished him a polite good morning before returning to the game app on her smart phone. She was shown into the office, leaving David alone.

Ten minutes later, she left, and the receptionist took a call on the desk phone before telling David to go right in.

Dr Walters rose to greet him. Her handshake seemed warm enough.

"Do I sit on the couch?"

He asked, almost sarcastically.

Ruth smiled and replied

"I suppose, if you wish, but I would prefer you sat here. I just want to talk at the moment. Tell me about yourself, not your job. I know you are a constable. What I would like to know is what things worry you, or scare you; say politics, or your relationships?"

"You mean with my wife?"

"Not especially any relationships. I think I am correct in thinking you do not really want to be here."

David now smiled

"Is it that obvious?"

"Well, the fact that your father-in-law made the appointment was a bit of a give-away."

As the interview progressed, David relaxed. Ruth was easy to talk to; she had a way of putting him at ease. They spoke for about 5 minutes, and then Ruth asked the question he was dreading.

"So, about these dreams, can you remember anything about them, maybe a setting or a name?"

David had tried on several occasions to recall, but had failed.

"That's just it; I wake up scared, thrashing around. Debbie tells me I cried out the name Joan at one time, but it's crazy. I don't know anyone called Joan. All I can remember is being so terrified, trapped if you like, unable to breathe."

"Actually, David, such dreams are more common than you think. The reasons for them vary wildly. I would like to try a simple word association test. You understand what that is?"

David nodded

"You say a word, and I repeat the first word I associate with it."

Ok, it's important that you say the first word that you think of, regardless of how crazy it sounds.

Ruth turned on her computer monitor. The computer screen displayed the questions, but Ruth had angled it so he could not see them. Then she began.

Q; "Love"

A; "Debbie"

Q; "Hate"

A; "Spaghetti"

Ruth smiled but continued

Q; "Dog"

A; "cat"

A; "Joan"

Q; "Of Arc. Sorry, that was two words."

Ruth persisted

Q; "Danger"

A; "Ship"

Q; "Water"
A; "Fall"
Q; "Swim"
A; "Can't"
Q; "crew"
A; "Gone"
Q; "Gone"
A; "Black"
Q; "Family"
A; "Gone"
Q; "Time"
A; "gone"

Ruth had noted his answers and saved them before closing the screen. Then she turned to face him.

"What's the earliest memory you have in your childhood?"

David thought for a moment.

"The house; a poky little house with a straw roof, sorry, thatched roof."

"Your house?"

"No, another one, not sure whose, or even where, I asked my parents, but they couldn't remember one either. Maybe I dreamed it."

Ruth nodded, as if in agreement.

"Ok, let's go back to these nightmares. I know you say you cannot remember details, but I understand from what your wife told your father-in-law that they were very frightening. What I want to know is how frightening, and by that, I mean what form. Some people fear being alone; others of failing badly, then there are the darker kind. Fear of the unknown, fear of being trapped, or helpless, fear of death. Do you follow me?"

David did, and was becoming suspicious, but replied, though cautiously.

"Well, it's more of the latter, a feeling of some impending disaster that I am powerless to stop. In real life, when I have a problem, or obstacle, I

can usually analyse it, and see a solution. But in the dreams there is no solution, or more accurately, I lose my power of reason."

Ruth nodded and then began asking more general questions. About home, and what it was like being a police officer. David failed to see the relevance, but Ruth was putting him at ease. Finally, she said to him,

"Alright David, I want to try something. I want you to get comfortable, try the couch, and just relax."

David smiled and played along. He thought to himself 'If she thinks she can hypnotise me; she is in for a shock'. But he complied.

"Alright David, I want you to close your eyes and try to clear your head, concentrate on your heartbeat and listen to it, listen to my voice and try to answer questions I ask you. And don't worry; no one can persuade you to act differently to me, or act differently than you do normally. Despite what you may have heard, no one can control minds, OK?"

Ruth was good at her job. She knew the easiest subjects to hypnotise are those that are convinced they never could be; because in the depths of everyone's mind, there is just the faint suspicion that they could be.

Ruth waited about two minutes before beginning.

She switched on the recorder.

"David, can you hear your heart?"

"Yes"

"I want to take you back in time, back to when you were a child. You are playing with your friends"

"Yes"

"What are you playing?"

"Cops and Robbers"

"And you are the cop?"

David's voice changed. He now sounded like a young, smart assed kid, like so many she had known growing up.

"Nah, coppers are queers. I'm Ronnie Biggs."

"*So what do you do, Ronnie?*"

"*Robs trains dun-ni.*"

"*Alright David, now I want you to relax. We're going back further, back long before school, back into the darkness. Now we have stopped. Where are you now?*"

David did not answer at first, then replied in a deep accented voice she did not recognise, almost Shakespearean.

"*Got me a job, Archer on the Rose, good pay, 'Tis too.*"

"*What's the Rose David?*"

"*Where you been, madam, Henry's ship, The Mary Rose.*"

Ruth stopped. This was not making sense. Although she had heard of past life regression during hypnosis, Ruth also knew it was debunked science. The investigators found that all the cases were fabricated by the brain, so it was likely that his brain had remembered some comment or news item when the Mary Rose wreck was discovered and raised in 1982. Ruth returned to the session.

"*David, what year is it?*"

"*Year of our lord 1545.*"

"*Tell me, can you see the Mary Rose?*"

David's voice became quiet.

"*She big and solid, solid English Oak. Just had extra guns fitted. The Frogs will turn tail and run for it. I Told Joan not to fret; the Frogs won't dare take on King Harry.*"

On hearing the name, Ruth looked up.

"*Who is Joan David?*"

"*Fair Joan, sweetest wife a man could desire, so she is.*"

Ruth paused for a moment, unsure of whether to continue the session. At the moment, David was calm; his voice had changed, but only in its accent. It did not appear he was acting of faking anything.

She continued, all the time carefully ensuring the recorder was running.

"*Tell me about your home. What's it like?*"

A smile came over David's face, and his tone became softer.

"Taint nothing special, two rooms and the loft. But it's enough for me and Joan."

"Tell me about Joan. Describe her."

"She is a comely woman, that's a fact. Don't see what she sees in me, but I love her like she was the queen herself. We don't have much. But I did give her a ring for her birthday. I traded for it with Joe Hawkins, so I did. He got it in Calais, France, real pretty twas. Green emeralds, or so he said. Belonged to royalty, he said. Not sure he was being straight with me like, but twas was pretty, so I traded my old bow for it."

Ruth paused for a moment. She wanted to test his story for details and would use them later, when David was not under hypnosis, and try to understand what was triggering these memories.

"So if you traded your bow, what will you be using in the coming battle. Surely an archer needs a good bow?"

"Made me a new one, pretty, solid, and cut from fine French mountain yew. It won't break, and in any case, the Rose has plenty of spares on deck. Funny, Joan asked me that, she don't know too much about navy ships, and that's good. Don't want her fretting none."

"But she liked the ring?"

"She said it was the sweetest gift in the world, and she would never take it off. She said it would be a token of our love. Real pretty with words is Joan, Real pretty."

His voice trailed off, and he seemed to relive a fond memory. Ruth decided to wake him and continue the interview in the present day. She needed to test something he had said earlier.

"Alright David, can you still hear your heartbeat?"

"Yes,"

"Good, now concentrate on it, and think only of how quiet and peaceful things are. Now I'm going to count slowly to ten. We are going to come back to today, back to your appointment with Dr Walters. One...

two... three... four... five... six... seven... eight... nine... ten. Can you hear me?"

"Yes, sorry doctor, I think I must have nodded off. This couch is almost too comfortable. I apologise; I don't think I can remember what you last said."

"It is common, no apology needed. While you were asleep, did you dream?"

"Can't remember dreaming, to be honest, can't remember falling asleep."

Ruth smiled and told him to relax. She had many questions, but gave him a minute to re-familiarise himself before continuing.

Ruth knew her job, and this case was going to be a challenge. It seemed as if David was actually recreating a former life, right down to a unique accent and details. They spoke on other matters, what David would have termed low ball questions, before she got to more important matters.

"You remember telling Debbie about a documentary that was on TV the night you fell asleep in the chair and you had another nightmare?"

Surprise crossed David's face.

"Vaguely. How did you know about that?"

Ruth smiled

"She mentioned it to your father; he told me when I asked if you ever watched anything disturbing on TV, he told me you were a sports fan and did not like dumb stuff, so I wanted to explore that with you."

David shrugged.

"Well, he was right about being a sports fan, and right about that piece on the Mary Rose. That sort of thing doesn't really interest me. Oh, I know it's cool about finding such an old ship buried in the mud and all, but I've never been an avid history fan. I know about the war and stuff, from my parents, and their parents, but that's about it. The Mary Rose was centuries ago, Henry the Eighths and all that, wasn't it?"

Ruth nodded.

"The mid 1500s. I think it sank in the Solent during a battle. Tell me, do you remember any details of the documentary?"

David thought hard for a few moments.

"Well, not much. I turned on after it had started. I remember they constructed a big yellow cage to bring it up, and Prince Charles was there. They were talking about it being like a time capsule from the past. I remember thinking; anything in the ship would be pretty well sodden after hundreds of years."

He smiled, but Ruth continued.

"What sort of artefacts were they saying were on board?"

"Honestly, I can really remember. I think they mentioned a doctor's chest and some skeletons. Why do you think this dumb documentary had something to do with my nightmares?"

He chuckled at the thought

"No, I think it is unlikely. There are several things that might make you dream, such as a graphic, or violent, show watched before bed, but I doubt this documentary would have done it. Especially as you fell asleep during it."

Ruth thought for a moment, frankly she was running out of questions.

Meanwhile, in the small café outside the newly opened Gunwharf Quays, Debbie was opening up to her father on her fears.

"I do not understand this, any of it; David and I have had a splendid marriage. Why is he now getting these dreams? Do you think he has gone crazy, a brain tumour or something? It's just so scary?"

"For the record, I don't know, but I doubt it. David's problem seems psychosomatic, not medical. I would expect a tumour to produce headaches and such."

Her father did not reveal that not all tumours did so, and several sudden deaths he had investigated turned out to be tumours that were painless, and undetected until the autopsy.

Anyway, her peers hold a high opinion of this young woman he is seeing, and she is popular among them. I think if there is a solution, she may find it."

Debbie was not so sure

"And what if she doesn't?"

"Well, there may be another avenue that could help, but I think we need to see what Dr Walters comes up with first."

Debbie looked up

"Dad, you can't leave it at that. What other cause could there be?"

Her father took her hands and became very quiet.

"Well, we are assuming David is fantasising, but what if he's not? What if he is telling the truth, but doesn't realise it?"

....

Back in Ruth's office, she was becoming frustrated, but hid it well.

"Alright, tell me about what sports you enjoy, apart from football. I know you play for the force team, and are a Saint's fan, but what other activities do you do. Golf, swimming, or things like that?"

Well, I'm not ready for golf yet, that seems too leisurely for me, as for swimming, well I qualified in the pool at training school, but never had to swim in earnest, if you follow me."

Ruth nodded.

"In a lifesaving situation, you mean?"

"Yes, never had a chance to be a hero."

He smiled; Ruth thought she saw a trace of nervousness in his expression before continuing.

"How about boating, or Kayaking, has that ever appealed to you?"

"Well, I like fishing, sea fishing from a boat. Sometimes we go out from Portsmouth on a charter boat. I caught a big cod over a wreck in the channel last year; wrecks are good for big fish. They like to feed among the rusting metal and barnacles."

Ruth saw an opening and took it.

"How about the Mary Rose wreck? Did you ever fish that?"

David Laughed

"Hardly. She wasn't there, and before the salvage operation, the site was off limits. No one ever talked about fishing that wreck; it was raised when I was just a baby. Anyway, it was a wood ship, no metal, nor especially attractive to fish."

Ruth thanked him for the session and asked him to make another appointment the following week. Two more sessions followed, each more bizarre than the last. The problem was, that the sessions were not getting anywhere fast. She knew she needed help on this one, and knew the very person to approach.

Chapter 3

Doubts

"Come in Ruth, nice to see you again. How's the practice going?"

Ruth smiled and took the extended hand of her former professor, Sir Michal Walker; a former Harley Street Psychologist, and now a leading lecturer at the institute of Psychiatry, Psychology, and Neuroscience at Kings College London, from where Ruth had graduated just two years ago. She had asked to see him regarding David's case. Certainly not the first student to do so, but he usually answered such requests over the phone. In this case, he had agreed to meet his former student. She had been a particularly gifted student, and her call had intrigued him. He had recalled her interest in past life regression theories, and the fact she had brought tapes with her would give him more case material to share with other students.

"So, what intrigues you particularly about this case? You mentioned past life regression, well as you know, such cases usually have a foundation in everyday events. The human mind is an incredibly complex organ. No modern computer has been able to replicate its functions. But I recall we had this discussion many times. In fact, my students still bring it up."

Ruth smiled and replied,

"Well, David's case is puzzling. He does not appear to recall anything following our sessions; and speaks as if he is relating incidents in real time. Most times I've heard of choose someone famous like a king or princess, or they have inside knowledge, such as an interest in the period, David does not. In fact, the last thing he would want to be made public is his consultations with me. As a police officer, he feels it would jeopardise his job. Whenever I mention The Mary Rose, his is indifferent, and says he

32

recalls something about it being raised on a TV show recently, that he actually fell asleep during. He could recall nothing of the program in detail."

Professor Walker nodded.

"But he is quite lucid under hypnosis?"

"Very. He has a clear and precise memory, or assumed memory of details, descriptions, and people, not famous, just his wife and crew mates on the ship."

"And you have not discussed his regression with him in detail?"

Ruth shook her head

"No"

"Why not?"

"Well, I wanted to ensure anything that I had said did not influence him. He has not, so far, questioned me about his hypnosis, but he is showing signs of frustration."

"Do you have copies of these tapes?"

Ruth nodded

"Yes, I thought you may want to study them at your leisure."

"Thank you, I would. Do you have any appointments pending with David?"

"Yes, in a week's time. Quite frankly, I'm not too sure where to go from here, so any suggestions would be welcome."

Sir Michael sat back in his chair for a moment.

"Well, first, I agree you should not, at this stage, openly discuss regression outside hypnosis sessions. To do so may trigger him to research the subject himself and look up the history of the period. I find that is a sure way of clouding the issues. "

"You mean he may start remembering what he has read rather than what he is experiencing?"

"Exactly so. Do you have any knowledge of this period of history?"

Ruth smiled, almost as if she could read the professor's mind.

"Well, to be honest, not much; but since I took this case, I have been reading up on it. Google is a mine of information."

"Indeed, so, in my day, I had to rely on massive volumes of medical thesis written by theorists who, well, just theorised. Today, students just punch in a subject on their iPad, and it's there. If you punch in past life regression, you'll get the king's collage library full of so-called proof of afterlife existence, written by some failed academic who wants to cash in on people's fears. Particularly those who have recently lost loved ones. Pretty sordid."

Of course, Ruth knew the truth of this statement, having done some research herself on the subject. To say the Professor was a sceptic would be an understatement. She chose her next question carefully.

"So, are you saying that true after life regression is a total myth, proven conclusively?"

Sir Michael smiled.

"No man can say that conclusively, Ruth. There are more things in heaven and earth than were ever dreamt of in your philosophy."

On seeing the puzzled look on her face, he added,

"Shakespeare's, Hamlet to Horatio."

Ruth understood.

"You surprise me professor, I thought academia had long rejected the idea as junk science."

"Well, that's true. I would say it's 98% rubbish, but it's the remaining two per cent that worries me. Maybe someday we will uncover irrefutable proof of the continuance of the soul after death, but we are far from there yet."

....

Professor Walker sat back in the comfort of his study that night. He was a man of great experience, and he had great respect for Ruth, who had a young and enquiring mind. Others may have gone all out on the largely debunked afterlife and regression theories, but Ruth had not done so. She had a question and was looking for a rational answer. The trouble was, as the tapes went on, such a rational solution seemed to get further away. This young man seemed to actually believe he had been a crewman on the Mary Rose, a ship that sank over 400 years ago. The obvious answer was that he had studied the ship and its crew in great detail, and was lying to Ruth, when he said he had no interest in her, but if that was the case, then what about his wife, and in-laws? Plus his parents, and if it was all a massive hoax, what would be the motive. One particular section of the tapes caught his interest. He rewound the tape and listened to it again.

"*Now David, tell me more about the ring, the one you bought for Joan, the emerald ring.*

"*It was beautiful, so it was royal, so Jo tole me. From the king of France, or someone like that. I asked im that, he said it was English, an English queen.*"

"*Do you know which one?*"

"*Secret, can't tell, he sid mustn't tell, dangerous to speak of such things*"

Professor Walker stopped the tape. Why the reluctance to name a queen? Why is it dangerous to speak of such things? And, on a broader plain, why the details? Why so precise? Usually, people experience convoluted and irrational false memories and dreams. What was going on in this young police officer's mind?

These, of course, were the same questions that Ruth had, but had not shared with Sir Michael. However, try as he might, he just could not accept the alternative. It flew in the face of reason.

....

At the time this meeting was in session, David had been back at work, on his way to North Walls, in Portsmouth. He had been attending a Post Mortem on a young druggie who had been discovered dead by his girlfriend. Routine stuff, but the CID had to go through the motions. As he walked into the office, his supervisor, DS Harper, looked up.

"*Any Problems, Dave?*"

"No Sarge, just another toe rag who shot up one time too many. The Coroner says we'll have toxicology in a couple of days, but he seems pretty sure it was heroin."

Harper shook his head.

"Total waste, still, one less to worry about. Oh! Speaking of toe rags, one of your CROs was in earlier, Peter Fuller, remember?"

(CRO - Police jargon for Criminal Record Office Subject)

David smiled briefly.

"What was he nicked for this time?"

Harper laughed.

"Surprisingly nothing, at least nothing we know of. He wanted to see the Vulture."

An icy feeling suddenly came over David, as he pictured Fuller, and now remembered the face in Ruth's waiting room. His imagination went into overdrive.

"Did he give any reason?"

Harper Shrugged.

"Said it was personal. The SDO said she notified him, and he was with him for about 5 mins, but I've heard nothing yet. Perhaps he was looking to join up."

(SDO - Station Duty Officer)

David smiled, trying to mask his concern.

"Probably fit right in with some of the latest recruits we're getting."

He knew there could be a hundred reasons Fuller would want to see Superintendent Hawke, other than seeing him at Ruth's surgery, but he had a gnawing feeling he was the reason. By the time his shift had ended, he had formulated a plan. He had brought up Collators' records of Fuller and his associates. One name caught his eye: Melanie Martin. She was an on - off girlfriend, and had a conviction for possession when she was 16, but nothing recent. The Collators file contained all known information, including, but not limited to, criminal associates or criminal records. He did not know her personally, but she could be useful. First, he decided to lay a false trail. He knew Harper was a reliable conduit to the Superintendent, and would report anything to him that would keep him on his side. To the outsider, this was a fact that made him untrusted with confidential info. However, it could also pass info to the chief, which was to his advantage, but without speaking to him direct. All Officers knew this, and the grapevine worked well.

At 5 PM, he put on his jacket and spoke to the Detective Sergeant.

"Ok that's me, done for today, got some homework to do on a case that may pan out later."

Harper, bit

"Oh really? Anything special?"

David shook his head.

"Not really, trying to get some info on the mental background of a kid whose parents think he's acting strange. Probably not amount too much, but trying to get official comment from the shrinks is like butting a brick wall."

Harper smiled

"Ok, well, let me know if you need anything. I may be able to call in a favour with the Hospital."

David felt satisfied that he had given Harper, and through him, the Superintendent, a reason for him being at Ruth's office. He covered that base. He cancelled his next appointment with Ruth, rescheduling it for two weeks later.

Ruth's interview with Professor Walker had gone well; he had offered several very plausible reasons for David's condition. But she still did not find herself convinced. She knew little more about the Mary Rose than he apparently did, so it was time to remedy that. At home, she turned on her laptop and typed in 'Mary Rose Ship'.

Then she settled in and began reading.

....

It was late when David's car pulled up outside the house. Debbie had been waiting nervously for him, and naturally wanted to know how the session had gone, but she also knew it could be a very touchy subject.

She kissed him lightly on the cheek as he entered the hallway.

"So, how was your day?"

David smiled nervously before answering.

"Well, to be honest, I'm not too sure about this entire session. And today, I saw one of my toe rags in Doctor Walter's office. Later he showed up at the station asking to see the Vulture. Maybe a coincidence, but I'm thinking this is going to backfire on me."

Debbie shared his concern.

"So, why was he at the station?"

"He asked to see the Vulture; wouldn't say why, but I think he was looking to make trouble."

"Well, did the vulture say anything?"

"Not to me, and not to Harper, as far as I know. But nevertheless, it's a worry."

Debbie could see that most of the worry was parking itself squarely on his shoulders. She also knew that there was little she could do to help, at least not with the threat from the force. She kissed him lightly on the forehead and smiled.

David looked up at her.

"Well, I guess there's not much I can do about it. I'm gonna take a bath and have a soak. Need to get the smell of the mortuary off me."

"That I can understand; G28s always leave me feeling unclean. I'll run it for you."

(G28 - police slang for a sudden death enquiry named after the report form number)

Unbeknown to him, the Superintendent had asked Harper later if he knew what David was working on, and been told that he was trying to get some mental background on the girlfriend of a suspect, but knew little else. That had seemed to satisfy him. However, Harper remained unconvinced.

....

Meanwhile, Professor Walker had come to the end of Ruth's tapes. He could see why she had come to him. Most past life regressions resulted from a latent memory or experience, a book read, or a job, or worry; the brain often had difficulty in evaluating this and sometimes produced a jumbled story that made no sense when analysed in the cold light of day. Following this logic, David should be regressing to his past, maybe mixing a childhood experience with his police career. That was easy to evaluate. The Mary Rose connection may make sense if he had been a historian, or a Navy man. But David genuinely seemed to have no connection or interest in the subject. Also, the recollections were not jumbled; they were coherent and visually stunning. The subject seemed at ease and describing actual events. The big question was, why?

....

David was at last beginning to relax. The warm bath had had the desired effect. He knew Debbie would want to know about the session, and he had not told her that he had cancelled the appointment with Ruth. He was all too aware that this problem, whatever it was, would be unlikely to go away. Ruth had not discussed the hypnotherapy sessions with him, but she had seemed to be strangely interested in that stupid documentary he had seen, or rather half seen. He knew vaguely that the bathroom door had opened. He opened his eyes to see a naked Debbie enter, and sit provocatively on the side of the bath. She was holding two full champagne glasses, complete with cocktail cherries.

"I thought you could do with a stiff one lover."
She said, with a twinkle in her eye.

He thought of the perfect reply, but decided not to air it. He took the glass and sipped it, and just smiled. She put the glasses down and kissed him, strong and passionate.

"I'm feeling lonely tonight David, how about you?"

David could not understand the change that had come over her, but it didn't seem to matter.

"What about the dreams? What if I go loopy again?"

Debbie placed her finger over his lips.

"No worries darling, I'll keep my ASP under the pillow."

(ASP - Armament Systems and Procedures, a Tactical expandable police baton)

....

Chapter 4

Reaching Out

Margaret Soper was another person troubled by dreams. A young parapsychology student with one published book, and that was under a pseudonym, she was not exactly a household name. Margaret was a student at the same faculty as Professor Walker; but had developed an obsession with the theory of life after death, after reading an account of a case in a book, 'The Airman Who Wouldn't Die'. It regarded the supposed spirit of an R101 airship designer that had involved the famed author and spiritualist Sir Arthur Conan Doyle. An obsession, she had decided not to share with her lecturers, who she knew dismissed the whole idea as pseudoscience. Recently, however, she had experienced disturbing dreams, which revolved around a woman who she did not know, but who seemed to intrude into her dreams regularly. The dreams never varied. In a state of agitation, the woman insisted that Margaret deliver a message for her. The problem was, she never got round to delivering the message, and could never remember who it was for.

She had confided in her boyfriend, however, a fellow student, Ian Farnsworth, who, though not sharing her belief totally, was at least willing to discuss the theory. He had helped her with her book, particularly the title, 'Have you lived in another time?'It was a catchy title that aimed to make a potential reader stop and give it a second look. She had carefully worded her authors' bio on the back cover to make it sound more professional, claiming no academic or scientific qualifications. For example, she had described herself as being a long-time student of parapsychology and the unknown.

Few looked beyond this bio to discover the real person. Or the actual job description of what a parapsychologist did. That suited her, and royalties from the book, though not huge, had helped with her college fees, and were now helping her at university. This situation would no doubt have continued uninterrupted, had it not been for the dreams. They were a constant source of irritation for her. She had often gone to sleep during the last few weeks, knowing she had to be more expressive. Asking the woman the name of the intended recipient of the message never seems to work. The dreams did not have any connection to real life, so each encounter felt like a fresh experience, with no sense of déjà vu.

The breakthrough came early one morning when her phone rang unexpectedly. It was her 6 AM alarm set for an appointment a week earlier that she had forgotten to cancel, and reset, and had therefore activated again. She rolled over in bed, cursing softly under her breath, but suddenly opened her eyes wide.

"Deborah Spencer, who the fuck is Deborah Spencer?"

She muttered as the sleep finally left her brain. As it hit her, the message was for someone called Deborah Spencer. Her mysterious woman had uttered it moments before the alarm. Quickly, she grabbed a pen and scribbled the name down, followed by rapidly scrawled notes of the dream, which was now rapidly fading from memory. She lay there, running the name through her head; did she know any Debbie's? Well, yes, several, but not with that surname. Had the name appeared in a film, or book, she had read. No longer able to sleep, Margaret got up and sent her boyfriend a text, resisting the urge to phone him and wake him up.

....

The news that Ruth received from her receptionist, that David and postponed his appointment, came as a relief to her. She had been on the point of rescheduling it herself. And it gave her more time to compare what she had been researching with the tapes of David's supposed regression. That research had revealed that 'The Mary Rose' was a Carrick type warship that had been in service to King Henry VIII's navy for 35 years prior to its sinking in 1545, in the Solent, between Portsmouth and the Isle of Wight. The cause of the sinking appeared to be a sudden turn that heeled the ship over, flooding its open gun ports. There had been a substantial loss of life, with most of the 400 crewmen going down on the ship.

Ruth had made careful notes of the construction and design of the ship, its armament, and on board inventory; little details that she could explore with David during her next session with him. Then she formulated questions that she could ask him under hypnosis. What was he wearing? What did he have to eat on board? Had he ever spoken to the captain? And so on. If he was telling the truth about the having no interest in the ship, these questions would reveal that his recollections were based more on assumptions than fact, a key breakthrough to her treatment for him. Of course, if he scored highly, then that was a different matter, effectively putting her back to square one. Of course, she could have simply visited the ship housed in a new museum within the Naval Dockyard, but that seemed too time consuming. Nowadays such information was instantly available on line anyway, and google had the advantage of enabling her to copy and print articles instantly.

The modern 21st century, she thought, this is the age to be alive in.

Meanwhile, Margaret had been busy with her own research. Using the same tools, she started by typing in the name Debbie Spencer, but that threw up millions of names and links. After an hour, she had made no progress when her Nokia cell phone buzzed, showing an incoming call from Ian.

She loved this little mobile phone. A model 8250 was the latest in technology, a present from Ian, and it lit up with a blue light when activated. It was very expensive, over 200 pounds, and she was one of the few students to own one, though some senior staff members did, notably Professor Walker. Ian's family was, however, well off, and seemed to have little money worries.

She thanked him for getting back to her so fast, and she outlined the dream and the name, but it meant nothing to him either. However, he agreed to meet her in the cafeteria for coffee to discuss it. She knew she would have to narrow the search somehow. Finding out Debbie's nationality would help, and the contents of the message may also provide clues. Privately, Ian thought the whole exercise was a total waste of time, but of course, he kept those thoughts to himself. However, he found himself mildly intrigued. If this Debbie girl proved to be a real person, and the message was really from 'the other side', then it would be a pretty cool event.

Margaret had studied the scribble notes and noticed the name Portsmouth. It was from her dream, but she could not remember who had said it. Ian stated that as far as he knew, Portsmouth was a naval port on the south coast of England, and there was one in America, too. He had a pen friend who lived there. He wasn't sure if it helped. It didn't, but at least he was trying. Then she remembered the old case that had got her started on this whole past life thing. She still had the book, but hadn't read it for years. It was called 'The Airman Who Would Not Die', by John Fuller. That was also about messages, so she dug it out and read it again.

For his part, Ian was unsure of how to proceed. He was smart enough to realise that if she got too much involved, it would have a negative effect on her studies, and may jeopardise her future career in the field of Psychiatric medicine. Then he got an idea. The coming weekend there was a psychic fair being advertised in London, an event that would not normally have interested him, but it may prove useful.

These affairs usually attract both believers and sceptics. It was an all-day event, and featured a famous clairvoyant, Liz McDonald; who was signing books and autographs. He surmised there would probably be other mediums there who may help research into past life regression. Coincidentally, his assumption would be correct.

To his relief, Margaret had been very keen on the idea. So Saturday morning found the couple outside the Shepherd's Bush Community Centre, where the event was taking place. On entry, there were the expected vendors selling crystals and scented oils. An Incense stick was burning, which Ian thought probably masked the trace odours of cannabis smoke. Still, the bulk of the hall contained several mediums that sat at tables, with black and gold name plates that identified them, and their particular specialty. None, however, appeared to be past life regression, but three, identified as spirit guides.

He left the choice to Margaret, and they approached the table of Mrs Caroline De Winter, a posh sounding name, that in reality, probably referred to a daytime cashier at Woolworth. Ian spoke first, trying to play it as straight as he could.

"Good morning Ma'am, are you free?"

De Winter looked up and smiled.

"No, young man, but very reasonable."

She extended her hand.

First impressions; De Winter was a refined woman, and had a distinct upper class accent that seemed genuine, and not contrived.

"My Name is Ian Farnsworth, and this is my girlfriend, Margaret Soper. We are interested in psychic research, and matters relating to the afterlife."

De Winter extended her hand and Margaret took it. The effect was electrifying. Her smile faded, and she stared for a moment before she recovered.

"I apologise, Margaret, but can I ask you something?"

They both sat down

"Of course,"

De-winter again took her hand and whispered.

"I believe you're not being honest with me Margaret, I believe the research thing is a smokescreen. Would I be right?"

Margaret began to splutter a denial and looked up at Ian.

"Don't misunderstand me, but I sense an inner struggle within you, dreams, I think, a recurring one."

Margaret shot Ian an accusing glance, but he shook his head.

Sensing her suspicions, De Winter moved quickly to dispel them.

"No, I assure you, no one told me, and I have not seen either of you before, but maybe I can tell you my take on the reason for your visit. If I'm wrong, then so be it."

But she added,

"I am never wrong. This recurring dream is disturbing to you, because it features a woman who you do not know, named Joan. You cannot understand who she is, and more importantly, why she is in your dreams. Right?"

Margaret was in shock.

"But how; how could you possibly know that? I never knew her name."

De winter looked back at her, more softly this time.

"I didn't know, not until I took your hand, but the communication from Joan Grainger was deafening. She is adamant that you deliver the message."

Margaret dropped her **scepticism**, at least for the moment, and replied.

"How can I deliver a message to someone I've never heard of? Do you know how many Debbie Spencer's there are on Google?"

De Winter continued.

"Actually, I don't, but even if I did, it wouldn't matter. Debbie Spencer is the recipient of the message. The woman in your dreams is Joan Grainger, and she died a long time ago, of that I am sure of. Her spirit is in you, and now, though, you, me too. You see, mediums, contrary to

popular belief, cannot call up the dead for a chat. There is no directory of their phone numbers. Mediums like me serve as channels for spirits to communicate messages. While in contact, we can communicate with that individual spirit, but no one else. Do you understand?"

Margaret was not sure that she did, but replied.

"Yes, I think so."

Ian put in his ten pence worth

"You're saying that this spirit has an urgent message for this Deborah woman, so why is she channelling Margaret? Why not a medium like you?"

De Winter shrugged.

"That I don't know, but there will be a reason. There always is. Look, this venue is not really the place to continue this. I would need to conduct a séance alone with just you and the Joan Spirit. Would you like to do that?"

Margaret was not sure if this was a good idea, and looked to Ian for his reaction.

De Winter saw this and interjected.

"Of course, your friend can attend too, but with some stipulations. The link will be between the spirit and myself. You, Ian, cannot question the spirit directly, and they may, or may not, want to speak to you through me. It is an aspect that is beyond my control."

Margaret nodded.

"So, where would you suggest we do this? Do you have an office or something?"

"Not really, but even if I did, you would be more than likely to suspect hidden recordings or projectors. It would be better to hold it at your home, where you know there is no jiggery pokery going on."

Margaret shook her head.

"I live in student accommodation, at Kings, not really practical."

Ian saw the chance to get back into the conversation and took it.

"My parents have a weekend cottage in the Cotswolds. I'm sure we could use it for the weekend. Would that be suitable, Mrs De winter?"

She smiled.

"Very suitable,"

She took out her planner and scanned the pages.

"Would next Sunday be agreeable? I have no appointments that day."

After a quick consultation, the two students agreed.

"Sunday it is then. Let me know the address. Shall we say 1 PM?"

Chapter 5

Night Terrors

Caroline De Winter was not a woman easily ruffled. She had been a normal teenager growing up, and had been dating a young soldier from the Royal Green Jackets. A roadside bomb killed him in 1978 while serving in Northern Ireland. That would have been traumatic enough, but at the time he died, she had a strong premonition and had tried to find out if anything had happened to him. That night, he had come to her in a dream, smiling and talking to her; she woke up in tears and knew he was gone. At first, she put this down to emotional shock. Her mother had tried to tell her it was a natural response. However, Caroline was not persuaded by her mother's explanation. The incident had opened a door for her, and she investigated the subject more deeply. That is what first drew her to the psychic fairs. There, she met other mediums. Most were unconvincing hippy types who wore headscarves, and often used tarot or Chrystal balls to assist them. She quickly learned to spot the fakes, concentrating on the others particularly, the authors, and the ones who could explain her growing ESP abilities.

That evening, she had concentrated on something the spirit had said to her, or more accurately, something that was in the background. Like a distant bleed over that you hear on the radio when the station is not close enough to get clear reception. She turned down the lights and began exploring her deepest thoughts. The voice came again, clearer this time, a man's voice; she tried to materialise him, but was only partially successful.

"Caroline, you must break the curse; stop it now, for the sake of those too blind to see. Caroline, the ring, the ring."

His voice faded. To any ordinary person, this would be an unnerving, perhaps even spooky, experience, but Caroline De Winter was no ordinary woman. She opened her eyes. The man's face was vaguely familiar to her. His clothes were from another time. For a moment she sat trying to remember what he said, exactly what he said. He had used her name. That could mean he knew her, or at least of her. But how could that be? His clothes showed he was from 2 to 3 centuries ago. He had spoken of a ring and a curse. The ring, why did that ring a bell, something from deep in her memory, from her past, her family's past? Quickly, she went to the computer, turned it on, and selected a folder marked 'Ancestry' from the desktop. She opened it to reveal the De Winter family tree. She scrolled down the chart, back down over the centuries. Then she saw it.

Francis De Winter 1514 -1544.

She clicked on the name and brought up the details.

Francis De Winter, Born London 1514, Business, jeweller in Calais, France

Married Evette Doubis 1532, two children, died, August, 1544, murdered by an unknown assailant at his shop. (Reputed to be the source of the family ring curse)

She remembered adding the note regarding the curse, but it was just a hand-me-down legend. That her grandmother had spoken of. The supposed curse placed on a ring by Anne Boleyn at her execution. It was supposed to bring death and unhappiness to whoever possessed it. The legend claims that Francis gained the ring and met his demise shortly thereafter. According to her grandmother, an English sailor bought the ring from his wife and died the following year. After that, it seemed to have disappeared. She knew there must be some connection with the ring and the voice in the séance. She descended from this English antiques dealer, but had little knowledge of him or his wife. Luckily, she had kept a file on her research into the family tree. Examining it gave some extra leads. According to the record, her ancestor died during an argument with a customer who stabbed him with his sword. He could not name his assailant after being discovered dying in the shop by his wife. He did, however, instruct his wife to dispose of the ring, as it would bring evil to her and the family. The record showed she had disposed of it to a man named J. Hawkins.

She closed the file. Many questions, but no answers. Maybe this weekend would turn up something more.

....

Relations had improved between David and Debbie after the bath incident, and the dreams seemed to ease, but they had not gone altogether. However, Debbie noticed they had become less intense

One night she awoke to find him panting and sweating, his eyes transfixed on the ceiling. She sat up in bed and touched his arm.

"Another dream, sweetheart?"

David turned to look at her.

"Yes, but not as scary. This time was about a ship, a big sailing ship, maybe a pirate ship. As a crew member, they sent me below decks to retrieve something, but I can't recall what it was. The door slammed, and I could not open it. I was banging, but no one was there."

"A pirate ship; like Blackbeard and the Spanish Main, Yo Ho-Ho, and all that?"

She was smiling, and he knew she was trying to put him at ease.

Finally, he smiled back. The dream was melting away, and he found himself back in Debbie's arms, which seemed to be all that mattered.

"Crazy isn't it, pirates, but maybe not pirates. Some of the crew had swords and looked pretty mean; still, who can fathom a dream?"

Debbie nodded

"Well, maybe your shrink can make sense of it? It could be important. Make a note of all you can remember about the ship and crew, and any conversations."

....

In fact, Ruth Walters had not been idle. At this time, armed with several hours of notes regarding the Mary Rose, and the time period of her sinking, she had prepared a good list of questions for David at their upcoming session. That was over a week away. Until then, she did some research on ESP and former life regression. Google had a wealth of information on the subject, but it was of little help. She divided the articles up into 3 columns; first the sceptics and evidence against, then the religious zealots, and third, those with no overwhelming explanation. It was the third column that most sparked her interest.

There she found many articles of experiences, some revealed under hypnosis that defied conventional science. Some articles strolled into the realm of dream interpretation. This was a subject she had some knowledge of. At this juncture, she thought about calling Professor Walker again, but chose not to inconvenience him, in case it ended up being unnecessary.

She received an unexpected call from him; a request, if she minded him sitting in on her next session with David. Of course, she felt delighted, but she knew she would have to set some conditions. First, the patient would have to agree. And also, the nature of the session would prevent him from asking questions of his own. Of course, the Professor knew this, and posed no objection, but suggested a couple of questions she might put to him.

It seemed as if the Professor was interested in this case after all, or maybe, and more likely, he was looking for more case histories to use in rebuttal. Either way, she was grateful for his insight.

....

Unaware of the events ongoing, regarding her husband's case, Debbie Spencer had called in on her father. Something had been troubling her, and she needed to speak to him. Her mother fixed the coffee, and she came straight to the point.

"Dad, David's dreams have become less severe in recent weeks, but they are still there, so I think the treatment is helping. However, there is still this underlying theme of being on an old ship. Sometimes he remembers snippets, and it appears to be an old sailing ship. He told me that a lot of his sessions involved ships, but he could not remember which ship or when. Do you remember telling me of the possibility of David not hallucinating, but actually telling the truth? Can that really be possible?"

Her father smiled.

"To tell the truth, kitten, I'm not sure. Do you remember the case of Peter Sutcliffe, the so called Yorkshire Ripper?"

Debbie looked up, a little surprised.

"Yes, he was the bearded guy who killed a load of women. Why?"

"Well, there was a man who helped with that case. Nella Jones."

Debbie shrugged

"Never heard of him. Was he a witness, or did he turn queens evidence and shop him?"

The Ex Chief Inspector smiled and shook his head.

"Actually, neither was his name made public. So I'm not surprised you've never heard of him. Jones is a psychic, claimed to have clues as to the rippers' identity. Oh, I know we can't convict on evidence from a clairvoyant, but this man could give uncanny information, including the man's first name, the type of work he did, and details about his company, that together with some good old-fashioned police work, led to his arrest."

"So, are you saying that this clairvoyant is the real deal?"

"No, I cannot say that, but that case defies other explanations. Now I've been a police officer for many years. I've seen and heard things that could not, on the face, ever be true, but following some digging, many turn

out to be so. People dream for a reason, and often that reason is a mystery to us. There are people who say they can interpret dreams, and some make a good living out of doing so. Nothing is ever quite what it seems. So what I'm saying is; it can be a mistake to dismiss evidence just because it does not fit your narrative. That's been the undoing of many a copper."

"So, where do I go from here, is that both Doctor Walters, and a Psychic, can see back into the past, but neither would accept the other as being credible, so they would likely argue over facts, and that helps no one, least of all David."

Her father smiled again at his daughter's simple logic.

"Well, I suppose it's a matter of faith. Now there are those that believe the bible is the word of god, and is totally accurate. Then there are others, the atheists, who believe men wrote it, as a guidebook for humanity. Both consider they are right, and both consider the other is wrong; they live a life on the line, and coexist. Now, I am far from being an expert on these matters, but from what I've heard, psychics reject neither religion nor science. They simply believe that there are things that happen that either religion or science can not explain.

....

While Debbie was talking to her father, David had other things on his mind. He knew that he and Debbie were having troubles, and saw the opportunity to set matters back on course. Next Saturday was their 3rd wedding anniversary, and she deserved something special. He knew that behind her tough girl image, Debbie had a soft spot for girly things, particularly jewellery. A fine necklace would suit just fine, nothing too pricy, but something that would impress her and her parents. He was not sure why that was important, but he recalled how anxious she had been to show off the diamond engagement ring he had bought her 4 years ago. So he headed downtown.

He found several high-class jewellers, which unfortunately for his budget, also had high price necklaces. At times like these, he needed advice, and on matters of gifts of jewellery, he relied on one person above most others. Detective Sergeant Christine Everett, a friend of Debbie's, and her matron of honour at their wedding, before her promotion, and he sought her out that afternoon. As usual, Christine had a shrewd idea that would likely solve his dilemma.

"Well Dave, first, if you buy something costly, Debbie is unlikely to thank you. She will probably dwell on the cost and feel you should have saved your money to help with the household budget. A better idea would be to buy something rare and unique. You will not find that in the high street. Try Fratton; there are several antique shops down there, and some pretty unusual pieces. They are unlikely to sell you anything bent, or try to rip you off if you show them your warrant card."

After his shift ended at 2 PM, he set off for the Fratton district in the north end. Christine had been right, after a couple of misses, he struck gold, literally. He explained to the elderly woman who owned the shop, that he was looking for a special anniversary piece; possibly an old Victorian necklace. After asking if she had a favourite gemstone, or birthday stone, and receiving a non-committal reply, the proprietor smiled. Most men had not a clue about such things. She went to a display case and pulled out a tray of rings. Most were gold or silver with various stones, but one seemed to outshine the rest. A gold dress ring set with 7 small emeralds, it was stunning, and looked early Victorian, not that he would know. He picked it up and turned it over in the light, trying to look as if he knew what he was looking for.

"Pretty isn't it."

The woman said, sensing his interest.

"It came in last month, from an estate sale."

David had to admit, the ring was striking.

"It's exquisite, Victorian is it?"

"No, it's much earlier, Tudor I believe, but probably a reproduction, based on what I paid for it at the estate sale, that's an actual piece of history you have in your hand, if only it could talk, eh."

David guessed it was going to be pricy, old stuff usually is.

"How much?"

The reply surprised him.

"Well, the market for Tudor stuff is a little flat these days; I can let you have it for 250 pounds. That is based on the gold and stone value. It would be more if it had some provenance, but all I know is the previous owner died and this was part of the estate. It did not come with any paperwork. Probably some rich woman in medieval times got it for a dowry or something."

David knew it was probably a fair price, and therefore most unlikely to be a genuine Tudor ring, but tried haggling anyway.

"Well, it is a nice ring. Could you accept 225?"

The lady smiled.

"No, but as you seem to like it so much, and I do have a soft spot for our boys in blue, I would go down to 235. That does not leave me much of a profit, either."

David smiled. This old girl was an experienced dealer, but no pushover, and seemed unphased by his job.

He held out his hand.

"I think we have a deal, madam."

David handed over the cash and accepted the receipt. Then, as an afterthought, he asked her one last question.

"I am a little rusty on antiques and such. How would you suggest I go about tracing the history of an item like this?"

"Hum! I think that may be difficult, even for a detective. I will tell you something that may help. Normally I would not divulge information of this sort, not good business, but the Ring was part of an estate sale handled *by Henry Adams auctioneers in Chichester. They may have details of the sale; I think it was last November."*

David thanked her and left the shop. He already decided to do some digging with the auctioneer. Figuring out if he could get some of the history behind the ring, it would impress Debbie, and if she didn't like it, then he may get a good return if he sold it. By the time he got home, he was feeling pretty pleased with himself all round.

Chapter 6

The Séance

It was 10:30 AM when Caroline De Winters' Gold Mercedes pulled into the drive at Keepers Cottage, on the outskirts of Calmsden hamlet in Gloucestershire. The location was picture postcard perfect, the weathered Cotswold stone façade, blending in almost perfectly with the natural stone landscape. This was no coincidence. County laws made it illegal to build in this area of outstanding natural beauty with any other material. She spotted the old Volkswagen beetle in front of the house and Ian and Margaret came out to meet her.

"You have a charming place here, Ian, quite a contrast to London."

The young student smiled as he held out his hand

"Well, actually, it's not mine. My parents bought it as a sort of retreat, and we borrowed it for the weekend."

Once settled into the living room, De Winter outlined the planned séance.

"Well, let me first say that there are no guarantees of success with any séance. I can try to establish a link with the spirit, but things do not always go the way we plan. I might fail, and another spirit, unrelated to this case, may contact me but wishes to converse.

Margaret had a question.

"Mrs De Winter, is there any danger in this ceremony? Sorry séance; I mean, can you call up a ghost or poltergeist who would not want to leave? I've heard of cases where people using an Ouija board have brought an evil spirt back to life, and it caused havoc."

De Winter saw the concern in her eyes.

"Well, there are no guarantees on anything. But I think this spirit is eager to contact you directly, almost to the point of desperation. So I am not too concerned about distractions. If, however, another spirit is present, I will sense it, and can to a degree suppress it."

Trying not to sound sarcastic, Ian chipped in.

"Sort of like saying, not today, thank you, and slamming the door."

De Winter smiled.

"Well, that's one way of putting it; however, some spirits have a habit of putting their foot in the door. So, are we ready?"

Margaret and Ian nodded.

"We have a quiet atmosphere here. We need that and subdued lighting. Drawing the curtains should suffice. "

Ian quickly complied.

De Winter sat down and closed her eyes. Both Ian and Margaret expected they would have to hold hands, but that was just for theatricals. She sat in silence for a moment, then spoke.

"Joan, are you there? You can speak now. I am listening."

Her eyelids flickered for a moment, then she spoke, but it was not her voice, though it was defiantly female.

"Too many deaths, too much heartbreak. I didn't know. How could we know?"

The voice was distinct; west Country, or welsh maybe, Ian linked it to a country bumpkin, no expression, but a sense of despair.

De Winter spoke softly, this time in her own voice.

"Tell us, Joan, what causes all this sorrow?"

"That damn ring, tis evil, it brings the devil in to our lives, we don't deserve none of this, it was just a pretty ring, the Devil's ring so twas. It needs to go back to hell so it do, straight back to hell. Tell Debbie she must destroy it or twill be the death of her and her sweet husband."

De Winter opened her eyes wide, staring straight ahead.

"Where is Debbie? Where can we find her and the ring, Joan? Can you tell us?"

There was a painful silence, then the spirt answered.

"David has it. It's a gift for her, a gift of death, *so tis, she must be warned.*"

"*Who is David Joan?*"

"*David's her man, her husband; he's giving it to her for their anniversary. He don't know. John tried to warn him, but he won't listen.*"

De Winter spoke again.

"*Who is John, Joan?*"

Her voice changed again as Joan came through.

"*My husband, he drowned, drowned, so he did, all cos that stupid ring.*"

Margaret couldn't contain herself and saw a possibility of getting an answer to a time-tested question.

"*Joan, is John with you now, in the afterlife?*"

The spirit ignored the question, and De winter continued.

"*Where do David and Debbie live, Joan? We do not know them.*"

"*David is a watchman, so's Debbie, odd that a woman watchman. They live in Portsmouth near the docks. So sure of his self is David, can't see the danger, thinks he's all high and mighty, but he loves Debbie as sure as I loved John. She don't deserve this, so you must tell her.*"

De Winter came back

"*I will tell her, Joan, we will find her and... Go Away. Be gone. I will not channel you.*"

Her Voice had changed, and she appeared angry

"*You have no right here, here...*"

Her voice changed again, this time male and authoritative.

"*Be silent wench, you do not order me to do anything; I will swat you like a fly.*"

De Winter came back with fire. Her eyes seemed to project anger.

"*There's nothing you will do. You have no power here; you are dead and buried, and remain so to all who care. You are nobody. Leave me and this realm, now. GO!*"

Silence returned. De Winter opened her eyes and glanced around. Margaret almost sensed fear in them. Finally, she spoke.

"Intense, and so evil."

Margaret was the first to speak.

"What happened? Why did you shout at Joan? I mean her spirit?"

De Winter sat back in the chair and sighed.

"I didn't. Joan gave us the information we needed, then another spirit came over, strong and evil, a sense of overwhelming evil. A man who wielded great power over men when he was alive, and cannot accept he has lost that power. I have encountered such spirts before, but not this intense."

Ian tried to sound positive.

"Well, at least you sent him packing. He won't be back."

De Winter smiled up at him.

"No, he has not gone, I wager. I will hear from him again, but spirits have no direct control over events in the living world. I think I can handle him. Now, let's see what we learned."

Margaret, who had been the only one to have had the foresight to make notes, looked at her pad.

"Well, we know that Debbie Spencer is living in Portsmouth and is married to a man called David."

"And they live near the docks; she said they were watch makers. So they are like clockmakers. Shouldn't be hard to narrow that down. Watchmaking is a dying art these days, so we could try the yellow pages."

De Winter said nothing, but seemed deep in thought. What troubled her was the apparent malevolent spirit that had intruded. That had happened before, but usually it was a spirit of a relative. This seemed different. She sensed an icy feeling of indifference, almost contempt. She sensed anger, and confusion in him, an anger that echoed down the centuries. A question from Margaret interrupted her thoughts.

"What do you think, Mrs De Winter?"

Caroline looked up.

"Well, I think we are making progress. But I do not think the couple in Portsmouth are watchmakers."

Margaret remained unconvinced. *"But she said they were, the spirit I mean, she said they were watchmakers."*

To ensure she did not kick off an argument, Caroline wound back the tape.

"Let's see, shall we?"

"David is a watchman, so's Debbie. Odd that, a woman watchman."

Caroline stopped the tape and shook her head.

"She said, Watchman, not maker. She thinks it odd for a woman to be in that profession, so would I in that era. The Watchmen were like the town criers. They walked the street at night to deter criminals, and reassure the citizenry."

Ian chipped in.

"You mean like a Bobbie, a Copper."

Caroline Smiled

"That's exactly what I mean. Debbie and David are most likely police officers working in Portsmouth. That should narrow the field down a bit."

....

Spurred on by the conversation with her father, Debbie was now beginning to entertain the real possibility that not only was her husband not crazy, but that someone or something was trying to warn him of something ominous. What that something was still eluded her, but she knew she had to find out. David was a straight, no nonsense sort, who she knew would dismiss any idea of spirits and warnings from beyond the grave, but she also knew he respected her father, not only as a senior police officer, but as a rational, deep thinking individual.

She was still evaluating these thoughts when she received a phone call from David's hypnotherapist, Dr Walters, asking if David could call her; she would not elaborate. Debbie reasoned that if it had merely been a request to reschedule next week's appointment, then she would have said so over the phone. Something else must have come up. Secretly, Debbie had longed to be present at the sessions, but David had always rejected the idea. He felt it was something he needed to keep between himself and Ruth. Fifteen minutes later, David got in from work, and she delivered the message. As he dialled the number, she sat trying to seem disinterested, but in reality, she was hanging on to every word.

She could not hear the questions, but David's replies made it obvious that she was asking permission for someone else to attend their next session. Finally, after he hung up, she couldn't hold back her curiosity any longer.

"So what's happening?"

David looked puzzled.

"I don't know. She wants a top phycologist to sit in on our next session, some professor from King's College. She said he's the top man in the field and could be of great help. I had to agree, but honestly, Deb, I wish the whole thing would just go away."

Debbie came to him and put her arms around his neck.

"Well, I don't see it doing any harm. Darling, for the record, I don't think you are crazy, or having a breakdown. There is something here beyond both our understanding. But whatever it is, it is real, and just ignoring it will not make it go away. Did Ruth give you any idea of what's happening or what you said, or told her, under hypnosis?"

"No, not really; I asked her, but she said she did not want to cloud the issue. However, she talked to me about the Mary Rose, the ship they brought up from the seabed some years ago. She seemed to suggest I may have kept some info from that old documentary that I was watching before I fell asleep."

She kissed him lightly on the lips and smiled almost provocatively, but was more worried than she was prepared to let on. Rumours were arising at work, some friends asking discreet questions about David, and if she was happy. They had started soon after a friend noticed the bruise on her cheek. As usual, Debbie had an answer, and put it to David one evening. The proposal was to host an anniversary party at the Netley police club. Their anniversary was not until September 17th, so they had two weeks to plan it. David thought it was a great idea and made the arrangements. As often was the case, he enlisted the help of Christine with the arrangements, who booked the club for the 15th of September, being the only free Saturday they had, and then compiled a guest list.

Chapter 7

Revelations

David's initial enquiries went well. The Auctioneers in Chichester remembered the sale and could supply details of the estate, including a copy of the receipt. David observed the item was categorised as a dress ring in the Tudor style, and he raised this issue with the auctioneer.

He looked at the receipt and said.

"That's not unusual; we did not get it valued because it came with a valuation certificate from the previous owner. We have that on file. Would you like me to check?"

David very much wanted him to check; minutes later, he returned and handed over the paper. A London Jeweller dated the paper back to 1943. The Heading was William Baker and Son, Bespoke Jewellers, The Strand London, WC2. It valued the ring at one hundred pounds, and described it as a reproduction Tudor ring, circa 1880.

The valuation seemed to confirm David's suspicion. If this ring was cursed, a star struck girl whose boyfriend had duped her into believing it was a royal king with a curse, was more likely to have done it. He smiled, well it was a good buy, and Debbie will love it, he thought to himself.

Halliwell Grange was situated 6 miles from the coastal town of Emsworth on the Hampshire, Sussex Border. Currently, it was owned by a leisure company who were renovating it into a conference centre. The former owners were the Halliwell family who had been in residence since the 1880s. A little digging on line, and checking census records, came up with 2 names, Charles and Samantha Halliwell, who had listed the auction, and now lived in Winchester. David sent them an email and asked for some information on the family history. He said he was researching an item from the sale, an emerald ring, and would appreciate their help. He did not reveal he was a police officer, deciding that may cloud the issue. Later that day he received a reply by phone.

Charles Halliwell was happy to meet him and could say, him and his sister had some information. At 7 PM that evening, David arrived at their home on the city's north side. Both seemed nervous, and for a minute, David suspected they may have known he was a detective. But the notion quickly vanished as they talked about the ring. It was Samantha who spoke first.

"The ring was my grandmothers, and I had forgotten about it until the valuers found it during the inventory. I remember her saying it had terrible memories of my grandfather; he had given it to her in 1940. The Battle of Britain claimed the life of my grandfather, an RAF Pilot. She never quite got over it. And never wore it again. I thought she had sold it, or disposed of it years ago."

Her brother chipped in.

"I spoke to her about it in the 70s, when I found it in a drawer. I thought it was Victorian, and we were doing a school project on the Victorian era. She told me it was older than Victorian, and she wanted to keep it. She had said, with a smile, that my grandfather had kidded her. It had once belonged to a queen, but I think he was probably just an old romantic."

David smiled at the mental picture of a dashing young pilot trying to impress his young wife with romantic tales of King Arthur and his knights.

"Do you have any idea where your grandfather got the ring?"

Charles shook his head.

"I don't think he ever told her, probably from a dealer in Chichester. While stationed at RAF Tangmere in 1940, he flew Hurricanes. I don't think we can tell you much more."

Samantha, however, seemed somewhat nervous, and finally asked what was on her mind since she read David's email.

"Tell us, Mr Spencer, if you don't mind me asking, what do you intend to do with the ring? Is it an investment?"

David could sense her apprehension, but totally misunderstood its meaning. He smiled at her.

"No, Miss Halliwell, I am not that mercenary. I bought the ring because it was very striking, and as a present for my wife on our 3rd wedding anniversary."

Far from reassuring them, his answer seemed to increase their unease. They both looked at each other.

David had seen this reaction before, in suspects that he had just advised to own up now and save harsher penalties in the future. Unsure of how to proceed, David spoke first.

"I sense you are not happy. Is there something you're not telling me?"

Samantha nodded.

"You should be a detective, Mr Spencer."

She turned to her brother

"Tell him Charles."

He nodded and responded.

"What my sister is referring to is the ring was supposed to be cursed, and would bring unhappiness to all who owned it. Our Grandmother told us she believed the curse because of what happened to my grandfather, but that was 60 years ago, and happened to thousands of other war brides. I don't recall any unhappiness in my grandmother's life since the war, so I would not place too much credence to it."

David agreed he had little time for such nonsense himself, but it made a good story. He thanked them for their help, and as he prepared to leave, he asked one last question.

"Do you know your grandfather's rank and unit at Tangmere?"

It was Samantha who supplied the answer.

Flying Officer Mike Halliwell from No. 43 squadron piloted his Hurricane, but enemy forces shot him down over Kent. That's really all we can tell you.

She added

"I'm sure your wife will love the ring."

David thought about where to go from here. There was a possibility that someone from Tangmere, who knew Halliwell, may be alive and could have more information. That night, he emailed the 43 Squadron association to find out.

....

Back at her home in London, Caroline De Winter was still unnerved. What had started out as a past life regression case had become more sinister. She had seen the figure of the evil spirit that had interrupted the séance. Not clearly, but well enough to judge his age and dress. It was definably medieval, possibly Elizabethan. High born and probably a man of significant influence, judging by his manner. She knew he was defiantly not the King, too slim, and had no full beard; possibly a member of his court.

Chapter 8

Challenges

David was a little apprehensive at meeting Sir Michael Walker. Ruth introduced him as an eminent Phycologist who had vast experience in the inner workings of the human mind. Sensing this apprehension, Walker extended his hand.

"I am very pleased to meet you Mr Spencer. My colleague Dr Walters has kindly invited me to sit in on this session, and I was most happy she did. Let me reassure you, that, I am here just to observe and learn. I've helped many patients that have unsettling dreams, and anxieties in my career. There is always a cause, and our mission is to identify that cause."

David took his hand

"Thank you, sir, for your time. I must confess I am as anxious as you to find out what is behind these dreams. To be honest, it has left me with a fear of going to sleep at night, and that is affecting my work."

The Professor nodded.

"I can see that would be a problem, and I assume the fact that your supervisors may notice this, and may also contribute to the stress."

Seeing the alarm on his face, Walker continued.

"My nephew is a police officer in Thames Valley Police. He once confessed to me, it's not good for one's resume, to have a shrink in the family."

His accompanying wink had the desired effect, and David felt easier.

After a few minutes, which allowed Walker to fade into the background while Ruth discussed his family relations with Debbie, and her reaction to his treatment; Ruth began the session.

"Now David, as before, I want you to close your eyes and concentrate. I want you to visualise a big old-fashioned grandfather clock standing upright, its pendulum swinging back and forth, back and forth. Each tick-toc will move us back, back into the past. The years are now rolling back across time; your marriage to Debbie, your school, and that frightening teacher, Miss Fawcett."

David's face showed a slight smile.

"Now back further back into the darkness."

She paused, studying his face.

"Alright, stop. What can you see?"

David remained calm, speaking slowly.

"Fair Joan, she has the sweetest smile. This morning I gave her the ring, twas a sight to behold. She cried, cried she did, I tole her not to fret none, but she said she was not unhappy, and she said she never got nothing like it, before, made her feel like a queen she said."

Ruth smiled at the visual picture the scene generated.

"This was the ring you got from Joe Hawkins. Tell me about Joe. What sort of man is he?"

"Oh, a godly fellow is Joe, nice with it like, but he would not fear to make a pretty penny, even from a shipmate. Least he speaks English, not like some of the others. Foreigners from faraway lands can't make head nor tail of the babble."

"So, where did he get the ring?"

"Who can say with old Joe? I think he got it in Calais. Tole me a great yarn he did; that it come from the executioner of King Harry's wife, the one that dallied where she shouldn't. That it were bad luck to have it, well I think he was trying to pull a fast one meself."

"Why did he say it was unlucky?"

"Well, twas for the man who sold it, got himself run through, after. Some say twas Joe that run him through, but eyes don't reckon so. Joe would only kill Frogs. This fellow was English, so I heard tell."

Ruth paused for a moment while checking her notes before continuing.

"You called your wife fair, Joan. That's nice. So what does fair Joan call you?"

David smiled

"Lately she's bin calling me Fair John, tis her lille joke, teasing me like, cos I calls her Fair Joan."

"So, John, you are an archer on the Rose. Tell me about that. Is it hard work? Is it dangerous?"

"Nah, not so as you notice, we are the top men, there Master Bowmen. They call us King Harry's secret weapon. The Fogs will learn that soon enough."

"So, is there a battle coming soon with the French?"

"Two days, they reckon. Maybe tomorrow if the wind holds, the frog fleet is coming up the channel. Got my orders to go tonight. Joan is a feared, so she is, but that's what the women are, they always think the worst. We will cover their ships in arrows like hail. I bet the frogs are shitting themselves tonight, make no mistake."

Ruth glanced at Professor Walker, who was grinning, before nodding for Ruth to continue.

"So, John, is this your first battle on the Rose?"

"First time since they fitted her out with the new guns and strengthened her. She's a solid lady, is the Rose. Hear tell King Harry is here in the city, to watch the French get whipped."

Ruth had not been idle since her first session with David, and now, through research, knew much more about the Mary Rose. Now she put that knowledge to use.

"So who's the Captain of the Rose? Have you met him?"

"Sir George Carew, a fine gentleman and seaman, he knows his ships, but don't have too much time for the crew."

"But I thought King Harry said you were the top men?"

"Oh, he don't mean us, tis all these foreigners, can't understand them, and he swears most have never been on a ship before. Reckon that's true, I seen one trying to row the skiff last week, gave us much merriment, twas a cause for much jesting."

The rough, unfamiliar accent seemed to come naturally to David. There seemed to be no attempt or emphasis in trying to maintain a front. Sir Michael knew many actors, some household names, and who were good friends. A good actor he knew could revert in to character quickly when prompted. But usually they simply re ran a script they had learned. This man was answering questions evenly with no prior knowledge of them in advance. That was more difficult. In short, he mused; if it was an act, then this young police officer was in the wrong profession.

The session continued.

"Right, John, how many men does the Rose carry?"

"Well, that depends. Mostly we have just the sailors, cept when we go to war. Amorrow when we sail, we will be fully manned with the soldiers and archers, as well as the crew over four undred spect, bow't the same as the Grace a' Dieu, King Harry is going board er tonight, glad it's er tho."

"Why, is that? Wouldn't you like to see the King?"

"Nah, not really, seen him once couple of years back. Want to spend tonight with Joan. She's so afeared."

Quietly, Sir Michael had got up from his chair and slipped a note into Ruth's hand. She glanced down and read it, then nodded and turned back to David.

"So, what's your full name, John?"

"John Grainger."

"And how old are you, John?"

"Not sure, bout 31 or two, spect."

"And how long have you been an archer?"

"Never bin notin' else, since I was knee high to a grasshopper, I spose."

"John, tell me about the Rose. What's it like on deck when you're shooting arrows at the frogs? Can you see them clearly?"

David chuckled, as if amused by the question.

"Nah, the boarding nets hide most of them. The secret is to shoot high in the air. The timing has to be right tho, otherwise you shoot over the ship, and hit the rigging and sails. I lob mine high, so they comes down straight and level, right on the decks. The Frog archers do that too, but they are no match for the master bowmen. Most time, we skewers em before they can get close."

"Alright John, I want you to relax, listen for the clock. Can you hear it?"

"Yes!"

"Now we are moving forward, back from the Mary Rose. You are back in school, playing Ronnie Biggs; now we are moving again. You are back with Debbie, you are now a police officer, as is she. The clock is about to strike. When it does, you can open your eyes and wake up."

For a moment, nothing happened, and then David opened his eyes, blinking for a moment. He looked at Ruth, then at the Professor, who approached and spoke first.

"I think, young man, we are making significant progress. I suspect that these dreams and nightmares are being caused by some deep-seated memory that we don't yet understand. But the good news is I think Dr Walters and I know where to start looking. How do you feel?"

"Well, to be honest, I'm not too sure, confused I guess; why would I fear suffocating, of not being able to breathe? I cannot remember ever being in danger like that for real, but I got these dreams when I was a kid; so my parents tell me."

The professor nodded.

"I believe you, but dreams of being unable to breathe are not usually to be taken literally. Mostly, they are an interpretation of what your mind feels. You feel unable to think ahead or understand what is happening, so your brain simplifies that emotion into a straightforward explanation.

Imagine you have a prisoner who is giving you a long and convoluted explanation of what made him commit a crime. You listen, but in reality, what he is actually saying is, alright, I did it. Do you follow?"

David did and appreciated the analogy. Though he was still not sure how it helped.

....

Three days after David had sent the enquiry to the RAF Squadron, he got a reply. Not from the association, but from a former member who had served with Flying Officer Halliwell, and co-incidentally lived in the town of Eastleigh, which was close by. He agreed to meet up with him at the local pub on the weekend.

It was 11 AM when David pulled up outside the Cricketers Arms, a picturesque inn close to Eastleigh airport. Keith Horn was just what you may expect a retired RAF type to be. A silver-haired man in his late 60s, and sporting a military blazer and RAF badge and tie. He Noticed David as he entered and called him over.

"I take it you're David Spencer, young man?"

Aware that these RAF types liked to keep their rank, David Nodded.

"Flight Lieutenant Horn, I presume, thank you for agreeing to see me. Can I stand you a drink, sir?"

Horn accepted, and the barman, who had already received instructions, came over to take the order.

"Right David, I must admit, I am intrigued why you want to know about Mike Halliwell; brash young man but he had guts, took on two - one o nines at once on his 2nd day. Most of us barely knew him. We knew he would either make it or get the chop. Unfortunately, it was the latter."

"Did you know him well, sir?"

Horn shook his head

"Not really. I was the squadron adjutant, had to do the debriefings, but he was a lively sort. I know his wife took his death very hard.

"Well actually sir, it's her I was interested in, really. I am researching an old gold ring that has an interesting history."

Horn looked up.

"A gold ring with emeralds. Was it supposed to be cursed?"

David found the revelation surprising.

"As a matter of fact, sir, yes, I'm trying to trace its history; you see, I bought it from Flying Officer Hallowell's widow via an estate auction. So far, the trail has reached back to 1940."

Horn smiled and took a sip of his beer.

"Oh, it goes back a lot further than that, old boy. It's Tudor, so I believe for four or five hundred years, I Shouldn't wonder. Mike told us about it when he bought it. About a week before getting shot down, Mike showed it around the mess.

Now that David had become well tuned in, he pressed on.

"Do you know where he got it from? Originally that is?"

Horn shook his head.

"Not really. He said he inherited it from a distant family member who died between the wars. He was apparently some kind of collector. Don't recall the name, but apparently he had got it for his wife. The story was that the fella that sold it to him was married to a Titanic Survivor, and was quite a woman, so Mike said. Personally, I think he was just an excellent storyteller looking for a better price. But I don't think I can be of much more help, really. I can't recall the relative's name, and all that may know, have passed on. I recall his wife was upset."

David almost smiled.

"Well, I would think so; it can't be easy to lose a loved one."

Horn shook his head.

"No, it was more than that. It was war, and we all knew our life expectancy was not good, but it went deeper than that. She told me at the

funeral, she blamed the damn ring, said she knew the ring was cursed, but didn't really believe it till Mike died."

....

While David was following up the leads in Eastleigh, Debbie was not idle. Unaware that David had purchased the ring, she was surfing the internet attempting to find any record of past life regression. At first, there seemed to be nothing concrete, a lot of speculation and cited cases, with little or no convincing evidence. In reality, she did not really know where to begin. David had shared very little of his sessions with her. She knew from the dreams that something was worrying him, but unless he was prepared to open up to her, there was little she could accomplish. But things were about to change when she got into work to start her afternoon shift.

The SDO spotted her and called out to her as she was signing in.

"Oh, Debbie, you had a phone call earlier from a Mrs. De Winter. She left a number."

Debbie took the in message form. The name did not ring any bells.

"Did she say what she wanted?"

The SDO looked sheepish.

"Well, not exactly; she said she needed to speak to the police, Officer Deborah Spencer, who is married to Officer David Spencer. I'm sorry; I confirmed that was you without thinking."

Debbie shook her head, more in understanding than anger.

"No matter. I do not think she would have left her number if it was not legit. I'll call her."

Debbie found an unoccupied interview room and dialled the number.

A woman with a distinct high class accent answered.

"Caroline De Winter,"

"Good afternoon Ma'am, this is WPC Spencer. I understand you wish to speak to me."

....

The session with Ruth and her patient had gone totally in an unexpected direction. After David had left the office, Ruth had been pretty blunt.

"Well, Professor, I think you can now see the problem I have with this patient. He does not seem defensive or irrational. He answered my questions about the Mary Rose without hesitation, and so far as I can tell, he got the answers right. If he is hallucinating, I cannot tell what is causing it. Previous cases of hallucinations easily debunked include monsters and persecution, but this one doesn't seem to have any obvious common denominator. What are your thoughts?"

Walker knew it was a great and pertinent question; unfortunately he did not have a ready answer.

After a moment's thought, he replied.

"I must agree. It is a very complicated case, probably the most I have ever encountered, and that in itself makes it more challenging. It is easy to just accept that there are still aspects of the human psyche we do not still fully understand. I know one of my students firmly believes in past life regression, has even written and self-published a book on it, and is unlikely ever to make a significant impact in the world of psychology. Nevertheless, it is good to examine such hypotheses.

"So, how does this student balance her belief with the accepted theory of hallucinatory imaging?"

The Professor smiled.

"Not sure. I haven't spoken to her about it; Margaret will have to work that one out herself."

....

Unaware of the events happening in Portsmouth, Margaret Soper was pursuing her own theory behind the manifestation of the spirit, Joan. She had dug out her copy of 'The Airmen who would not die' and began re-reading it, frequently stopping and underlining sentences and paragraphs. She noted that the medium involved had great difficulty in getting the subject of the warning message to take her seriously. That would also be a problem for her, should she approach this female police officer, who may suspect ulterior motives. That was why she had agreed to Let Caroline De Winter make the approach. Though she wondered what sort of reception, the medium would receive. She also noticed that since contacting Caroline, the dreams had abated. Maybe the Professor was right; it was just a psychological anxiety that was sorting itself out.

Chapter 9

Disaster from the Sky

Debbie Spencer was very suspicious of the mysterious Caroline De Winter; her conversation with her was brief, but pretty intense. She had told her on the phone that she had some important information for her, but had to see her personally. It was not unknown for police officers to receive anonymous tips of criminal activity, but this did not seem to fit the category. First, De Winter was not local. She lived in London. More importantly, she had said something alarming when Debbie had asked her what the information pertained to. She had replied; it primarily concerns her husband's dreams, and added, I think I may be able to help.

For this reason, she had agreed to meet her in Winchester at 1:30 PM on Tuesday, September 11th.

She had come prepared. A quick CRO check on Caroline De Winter with the Metropolitan Police had turned up no convictions. The Police had occasionally used her unofficially as a medium, according to their collator database. Armed with that knowledge, and regarding her earlier conversation with her father, Debbie had played it out.

Caroline was waiting in the car park in her Mercedes when Debbie arrived. She was 10 minutes early, but that did not seem to matter. Debbie shook her hand and got into the passenger seat.

Caroline spoke first.

"Thank you for agreeing to see me. I am sure if you are an excellent police officer, you will have run a check on me to see I'm not dangerous, and you probably know my profession."

Debbie smiled. She liked this no nonsense approach.

"It never harms to be careful in my line of work. So, what is it you wanted to tell me, ma'am?"

Caroline studied the young police officer for a moment. She was young, and she detected a hint of worry on her face.

"Would I be right in thinking that your husband has been experiencing some pretty unnerving dreams lately, about being trapped, and being unable to breathe? He has sought, albeit reluctantly, to consult the experts in such matters, but so far they haven't been able to help him."

Debbie became suddenly alarmed. This could well be a blackmail pitch against her. Her smile faded as she said;

"Go on."

"Well, the reason they cannot help him is that modern medicine refuses to accept the evidence of what they don't, or can't, understand."

Debbie replied with caution.

"Where did you come by this information, Mrs De Winter?"

"You need not worry Mrs Spencer; my source was outside both the police force, and the medical profession. The same spirit that is troubling your husband is also affecting others, including myself. It is a warning, basically a warning for your husband, and concerns a ring."

Debbie was now calmer and chose her next question carefully.

"Ok, supposing I believe you, what is this about a ring, and why should some dead spirit be concerned about it?"

"That, I am not too sure of yet, but I know it is important. The spirit voice is too strong to be anything other than a matter of great concern, I..."

Suddenly Caroline's voice trailed off, her eyes became transfixed, and she stared through the windscreen of the Mercedes, and her voice became panicky.

"God, No, for God's sake, Noooo."

She began to convulse and Debbie immediately grabbed her and shook her.

"Mrs De Winter, what is the matter, what is it?"

De Winter stopped convulsing and stared at her, but did not seem to be even aware of her presence.

"It cannot be happening, why is it happening?"

She was now sweating profusely, gone was the assured demeanour of a few minutes ago.

De Winter, had, had a severe reaction, most likely to drugs, though she hardly seemed the type. Debbie spotted a bottle of mineral water on the back seat and quickly grabbed it, unscrewing the top before offering it to her. Caroline grabbed it eagerly and gulped two mouthfuls, for a moment she said nothing, and then turned to Debbie.

"Thank you Mrs Spencer, Just give me a minute."

She sat back and turned on the radio then tuned to a classical music station and the melody seemed to calm her. Debbie spoke softly to her, all fears of a setup or trap had gone.

"Mrs De Winter, what's wrong, would you like me to call an ambulance?"

Caroline shook her head

"No Ambulance, no doctors, they could not help. Sometimes, having second sight is a curse that we could all do without. Something terrible has just happened, something unimaginable. Many, many people have died, and I saw it, God help me, I saw it all."

Now Debbie became alarmed.

"You saw it, where did you see it, what happened, when?"

Caroline did not reply, at first. Nor did she look at Debbie, but remained staring out of the windscreen, and then she spoke.

"Far away, far from here, it is beyond comprehension."

The music on the radio suddenly stopped. And a newscaster's voice replaced it.

"We interrupt this program for breaking news. A civilian airliner has just crashed into one tower at the World Trade Centre in New York City. The tower is on fire and emergency crews are responding. We will bring you updates as soon as we have them."

Debbie stared at the radio, then back at Caroline. As she realised what she had just witnessed.

"That is what you saw, wasn't it? You actually saw this happening 3,000 miles away?"

Caroline looked up at her, now revealing the tears in her eyes.

"No, not just that, I felt it, I felt the deaths of over a thousand people. And it's not over yet. Sorry Mrs Spencer, I think we will have to continue this at a later time. I cannot give you the attention you deserve at the moment."

Her voice had lost all of its earlier confidence. Debbie spoke, but her phone interrupted her. David's name appeared on the screen. She quickly answered.

"Yes honey, I know, I just heard. I'm in Winchester at the moment. I'm with someone. We'll talk tonight."

She hung up and turned back to Caroline.

"Mrs De Winter, I don't know about you, but I could do with a drink right about now, please agree to accept my apologies, and allow me to buy you one, no conditions whatsoever, Scouts Honour."

The last part was meant to break the ice, and to a degree it succeeded. Caroline smiled weakly and nodded. They left the car and walked to a bar, The King's Head in the shadow of the Cathedral. Debbie selected the lounge bar; they were the only customers and found a quiet corner.

....

By the time David had got home, news of the second plane hitting the Twin Towers in New York had broken, and all TV channels had moved to live coverage. David knew that Debbie was in Winchester and would not be back for a while, which gave him time to conceal the ring. With the TV on in the background, he picked up the box he had bought for the ring and opened it. It sparkled as the emeralds caught the light from the TV. Carefully he closed the box and put it in the inside pocket of his old uniform, hanging in the wardrobe. He reasoned Debbie would be unlikely to find it there. And if he knew his wife, she would guess there was a present somewhere, and would probably search for it. Once satisfied, he went back into the sitting room to watch the news coverage coming in from New York.

He wondered about the so-called curse, but paid it no heed. Now he knew the ring was not genuine. He reasoned it could not have been around at the time of Anne Boleyn. Pity, he thought, that would have really impressed her. After a while, he sat back and turned the volume down. He had been sleeping much better now, and the sessions with Ruth seemed to be helping. He closed his eyes and continued listening to the news, but the reports faded as he fell asleep. It did not last. His demon ghost returned within minutes. He could see her clearly now, and hear her desperate pleas. She was speaking to him directly, and telling him that Debbie was in danger, terrible danger, from the ring. He awoke suddenly and looked around the room. The TV was still blaring; angrily he shut it off and called out his wife's name.

....

Caroline De Winter was calmer now. The sherry had settled her nerves, and she again began to apologise for her actions earlier.

"Please Mrs De Winter, no apologies are necessary. If anything, it is me who should apologise. When I got your call, I was, shall we say, less than convinced you were the genuine article. My Father is a retired senior police officer, and told me the police often used psychics to assist investigations, and my checks on you showed a similar background. I was wondering just what it was you wanted to tell me. But the incident in the car told me you could not possibly have known about this attack in advance. In my book, that leaves only one explanation. In short, Mrs De

Winter, when you are ready, I am prepared to accept that you genuinely wish to help."

Caroline smiled.

"Well, thank you for that. I must admit that I was having doubts about how to tell you, without sounding, shall we say, a little batty. I do not know exactly how this matter involves your husband, but I'll tell you what I know; and before you reply, can I ask you that unless you are treating me as a suspect, or witness, that we drop the for formalities. I prefer to be called Caroline. Sounds less formal."

Debbie raised her glass.

"And you can call me Deb, or Debbie."

"Right, Debbie, best if I start at the beginning. About 3 weeks back, I was at a psychic fair in London, and two students came to see me. They were psychology students at King's College, and one of them, Margaret Soper, was being troubled by dreams. They featured a woman who kept insisting she had a message for someone of great importance. At first she could not recall the name, but later she remembered it as Deborah Spencer. After speaking with her, I could sense a strong psychic signature on her. From that, I arranged to have a private séance with her at a cottage in the Cotswolds belonging to her boyfriend's parents. During that séance, the spirit channelled me with the message. It did not make too much sense. But before I could get more information, another spirit that broke the link interrupted me."

Debbie was now paying total attention, and spoke up,

"Ok, I think I understand you, but I have two questions; first, did you ever get the message? Second, are you sure they intended it for me?"

"Well, yes, I got the message. Though it made little sense to me, I hardly expected that it would. The message was a warning about you being in danger because of a ring. As for identifying you, the spirit did that for me. She gave me both your names, and your place of residence, Portsmouth. She also gave your occupations."

Debbie took another sip of sherry.

"Well, that is confusing. I don't see the ring connection. Did your spirit give any clue what the danger is, and who may be behind it?"

"No, she didn't, and that is unusual. From what I could tell from her dress and speech, she was from a distant period in history, possibly 15th century."

Debbie's eyes lit up.

"The 15th century. Wasn't that the date the Mary Rose sank?"

....

The horrors of the 9/11 attacks were still very much in the mind of everyone as the guests assembled for Debbie and David's anniversary party at Netley. It was still very much the topic of conversation, and Debbie was hoping it would not dampen everyone's spirits too much. David, had so far, kept his investigations into the ring secret from Debbie, for obvious reasons. She had not told him too much about her encounter with Caroline De Winter, other than she was a medium who had contacted her, and she had checked out. Debbie knew her husband would be suspicious, and would likely check out the woman himself. Therefore, she had waited until the evening of the event to announce she had invited her to the event. As for Caroline, she overcame her wariness of the potential emotions that may arise with both David and Debbie in the same room because of her strong desire to meet David face-to-face, knowing he would never agree to a consultation.

David did not receive the news well; he had, of course, checked this woman out and found nothing sinister. On the way to the club, he voiced his concerns.

"I am not sure this was a good idea, to invite this medium woman to our event. Neither of us knows her, and I am worried she may spoil the event if she sees visions."

Debbie smiled.

"Seeing visions, god, honey, you don't know the half of it. When I met Caroline, she was just a contact that I had agreed to see out of courtesy. She had said she knew about your dreams, so I agreed to speak to her in a car park at Winchester, pretty public, so I felt safe enough. The meeting started well, then she changed, suddenly went into a sort of convulsion."

David interrupted, but instantly regretted doing so.

"Ok, so she's a druggie who speaks to dead people. This is going to be a splendid party."

Debbie stared at him with genuine anger on her face.

"Shut your stupid CID face for one minute. You may just learn something. This was no drug thing, believe me, I know a druggie when I meet them. This was genuine fear. She became scared and confused. She saw a great disaster, many people dying and screaming. I noted the time 2:15, that's 8:14 New York time. She saw the whole attack and felt the shock a full two minutes before it happened. It took me an hour to calm her down. I don't know this woman personally, but I accept she is genuine, so, not another word, right? I also checked her out with dad; he said it would be interesting to hear what she has to say."

Shocked, David said nothing. If Debbie was right, there was no other explanation. The enormity of that really affected him.

As they turned into the club car park, David spoke softly, having been keeping his own counsel for 15 minutes.

"Alright Honey, I'm sorry, l did not realise, maybe you should have told me earlier, but no matter, you have always been an expert judge of character. After all, you married me. I would be happy to meet this woman."

Debbie glanced around the car park, but did not see Caroline's Mercedes.

"Well, she's not here yet, so let's cross that bridge when it comes."

There was a cheer when Debbie and David entered the club. One of the first to approach was Superintendent Hawke., like most of the guests, he was not in uniform; but warmly congratulated them both, triggering a round of applause. Some guests were in uniform, and therefore, not drinking alcohol, but had their coke cans and water bottles, clearly on display, as they knew the Vulture was hovering. Christine, as ever, was on the ball, producing a glass of Martini, and Bacardi and coke, for the couple of the night. She proposed a toast, and the room responded with raised glasses. Debbie noticed a car pull into the car park outside the window, a gold Mercedes. She turned, still smiling to David, and touched their glasses together while whispering,

"She's here."

Caroline wore a fabulous dark blue trouser suit and looked stunning. The sight impressed David. This woman seemed a million miles from what he had imagined. As she entered, she drew many admiring glances; Debbie sensed the danger, and immediately crossed to her to ensure she did not start being questioned.

"Caroline, I am so glad you could make it. Did you have any trouble finding the place?"

Caroline smiled and replied,

"Not really. There was a police car at the end of the road, and the crew gave me directions."

David took a deep breath and approached as Debbie turned towards him.

"Sweetheart, I would like you to meet Caroline De Winter, an old friend of mine."

On cue, David extended his hand.

"Surely not that old a friend, Deb; unless you were at school together. I am delighted to meet you at last; Debbie has told me much about you."

The greeting seemed warm enough, and the three settled down at a table, joining the other guests, including Debbie and David's parents. By now, Caroline was still unsure of whether she had made the right decision in coming. She felt a little like Danial in the lion's den. After a few minutes, Christine joined them.

"Well Deb, what did David buy you for your anniversary present? Has he told you yet?"

Debbie grinned. She was sure he had brought the present with him, but so far had not revealed what it was. She had asked him, and been told, 'you'll find out tonight'.

"Not yet, but he brought it."

All eyes turned to David, who sheepishly produced a small ring box from his pocket and handed it to her.

"Happy Anniversary, sweetheart."

Debbie smiled and took the box. Carefully, she opened it. And her smile froze. After a brief pause, she removed the ring from the box, causing the guests at the table to gasp in awe at its stunning gold and emerald design. Except for Caroline, who stared incomprehensibly at the ring. Christine was the first to speak.

"It's beautiful; it must have cost a fortune."

David quickly replied.

"Not really. It's a Victorian reproduction of a Tudor ring. Had it been genuine, it would be worth thousands, but it's not."

Oddly, Debbie looked slightly relieved.

"You mean its paste?"

"David shook his head.

"Oh no, its genuine gold and emeralds alright, but not the top quality it appears to be. Made in about 1880 I think. But emeralds are Debbie's birthstone."

Debbie smiled and kissed him lightly on the cheek.

"Well, repro, or not, it's exquisite. And thank you, darling."

Noting Caroline's puzzled look, she handed her the ring.

"What do you think, Caroline?"

Caroline hesitatingly took the ring and stared at it. She closed her eyes for a moment before opening them. Both David and Debbie detected a look of shock, which quickly vanished as she realised being the focus of attention.

"It's a genuine work of art. Tell me David, how can you be sure it's a reproduction? Did you have it valued?"

The question seemed slightly rude, but David had no hesitation in replying.

"No, because it came with one from its original owner, and dated by a high-class jeweller in London before the war. And before you ask, Deb; No, you will not see it. Rest assured, I didn't sell the family silver to buy it.

The answer broke the ice as Caroline handed it back, whereby several others asked to see it.

Suddenly a voice called out for quiet. It was Detective Sergeant Harper. Once he had the room's attention, he called up Superintendent Hawke.

The Superintendent was still holding his wineglass.

"Thank you, Sergeant Harper, and thank you all for being here tonight. It is rarely that two married officers get to celebrate among fellow officers, and tonight I am happy to call a toast to two of Hampshire Constabulary's finest. WPC Deborah Spencer and Detective Constable David Spencer are living proof that a good marriage can survive the pressures of The Job."

The crowd murmured their approval.

"So, to Debbie and David, I offer my congratulations and best wishes for the future. Ladies and gentlemen, David and Debbie."

He raised his glass, triggering a crescendo of replies, *"Debbie and David."*

The guests quickly resumed their drinking and munching on the snacks Christine had so thoughtfully prepared. David had just circulated when he noticed a potential problem. Debbie's father was talking to Caroline. They seemed cordial, but she was the last person he wanted him to meet. Quickly as possible, without raising suspicion, he crossed to them. Geoffrey saw him coming.

"Ah David, there you are; Caroline is a fascinating woman. I've been so looking forward to meeting her, so glad she could come."

His response took David unawares.

"So, you two know each other?"

Caroline smiled.

"Yes, we do, but it's been a couple of years since we last spoke."

David felt puzzled. He knew Geoffrey was lying, but could not fathom why.

"Well, that's nice, I must confess. I had not heard about you till today, when Deb told me she had invited you, but it turned out to be a pleasant surprise."

Caroline was playing along. Something was going on that he could not fathom out. He was looking for a way to find out, but this was hardly the place. Finally, he made a move.

"Geoffrey, I have something on my mind I need advice on, do you have a moment?"

The retired Chief Inspector's reply was totally unexpected.

"This is Debbie's and your night. No need to spoil it for her with shop talk. Call me tomorrow. Remember, this was her idea to show how strong your relationship is. So circulate boy and show them."

David got the message; there would be time later to find out what was going on between them. He smiled before replying.

"Of course, it is not important. Will you excuse me, Mrs De Winter?"

And with that, he was gone back into the crowd. Caroline whispered.

"Thank you, Chief Inspector, though I'm not sure your son-in-law believed you."

Geoffrey nodded.

"He didn't, but he will not want to cause a scene. Fortunately, both of them are now on leave for a couple of weeks, so there's time to thrash it out. Now I'm no jeweller, and no little about gems. I don't think you are, but I read people well. It was obvious when you examined the ring, you did not accept David's word that it was a reproduction. Am I right?"

Caroline studied the floor for a moment before replying.

"Oh, I know it's not a reproduction. It is five hundred years old, and once belonged to Queen Anne Boleyn, a gift from her husband, King Henry Tudor. I also know that your son-in-law is not lying about its value, which is the problem. I am trying to reconcile the two facts. Not an unusual occurrence in my profession."

Chapter 10

On the Trail

Both Debbie and David had a tough time the morning after the party. Both individuals believed they were not being kept informed by the other person. David, understandably, wanted to know why Debbie's father had got information regarding Caroline De Winter that he could only have got from Debbie. Debbie believed he knew the ring was supposed to be cursed and had evidence that he had not shared with her. It left an awkward silence between them.

At 10 AM, Debbie called her father and was quite blunt, asking how he knew De Winter and explaining that David now suspected something nefarious was going on.

Geoffrey was his usual unflappable self, and asked her to come round and bring David if she could, so he could clear the air. It seemed like a good idea. David agreed, feeling that it was the only way to move forward. Their car pulled into Geoffrey's drive at 11 AM.

Once comfortably installed in the study, Geoffrey began.

"OK! Time for some clarity, I think. I think you've both been searching for an explanation of the unsettling nightmares and dreams that David has been getting. David has sought professional advice, but so far the results are not encouraging, Right?"

David nodded.

"Well, the world of psychiatric medicine is not an exacting science as such, although they are loath to admit it, there are some things that defy the normal rules of science."

Debbie now chipped in

"You mean the world of the mediums and all that?"

"Indeed, now that brings me to Mrs De Winter. Debbie, you remember kitten, me telling you about a medium the police used in the Yorkshire Ripper case called Nella Jones?"

Debbie replied

"Yes, you said she provided some useful information, but the police couldn't publicise it, for fairly obvious reasons. But what has that got to do with Caroline?"

"Well, I'm coming to that. When Debbie told me she was meeting her, I called a colleague who worked on the Sutcliffe case. De Winters' name came up as a medium with extraordinary ability, but she they deemed her to far away in London to be used, as the force would probably have to pay travel expenses, and that would likely raise eyebrows. They provided her contact details, and I called her last week. We spoke at length, and she said that she really wanted to help."

Debbie shook her head.

"So that's why you posed no objection when I told you I was inviting her to our anniversary party, and if I recall you said you were looking forward to meeting her, that's pretty devious, dad."

Geoffrey smiled but continued

"Well, as for you David. You have taken a more rational approach to researching the ring. You feel it must be a reproduction because 'A' it was so cheap, and 'B' because you have a 1940s valuation stating it to be a forgery. Sorry reproduction, right?"

David knew his assessment was correct, but was worried that Debbie would get the wrong impression. Therefore, he somewhat muted his reply.

And that I would not risk giving Debbie a ring that was supposedly cursed. She would blame me for anything that goes wrong in her life.

Hawthorne continued

"Well, Caroline has filled in some of the rings' historic past, so we know a bit. Also, you have done some recent history tracing yourself, David, tracing it back to the first part of the century."

Debbie now interrupted her father.

"So, does Caroline think this rings the same one?"

"In her mind, there is no doubt, which leaves us a mystery."

"Why is there a false valuation? For what reason?"

Chipped in David

Geoffrey nodded

"Exactly so. Of course, regardless of the answer, there is still the problem of David's nightmares. You may be interested to know, that one of Professor Walker's students at Kings has been getting similar dreams, involving what appears to be the same spirit entity, without giving her name, Caroline told me, as the student concerned has asked for her help."

Debbie now saw things more clearly.

"So Caroline knew this when she contacted me. Why didn't she say anything then?"

"For the same reason that you don't discuss cases with different witnesses until you are sure of the facts. Caroline knew she had an urgent message for Debbie Spencer, but did not know which Debbie Spencer. She was not sure she had the right one until she met you in the car park on 9/11.

Both Debbie and David were now thoroughly confused, and it showed. Finally, David spoke for both of them.

"So, where do we go from here?"

Geoffrey had been wondering the same thing himself.

"Well, you both have some leave, so you have no police work to cope with. I think it would be beneficial to get some more info on the history of the ring. And investigate more fully this valuation on it. Do you agree?"

Following the family showdown, the air was a little clearer. Surprisingly, both Debbie and David relished the idea of working on an investigation together. Whilst Debbie locked the ring away in the safe, David took another look at the valuation certificate. A check on the Jeweller concerned proved a dead end. The Blitz destroyed the building, and he couldn't find any trace of a new address for the company. Undeterred, he set out to research the history of the establishment and found records of its owner and staff. It turned out that the owner was a man named William Baker, who ran the business with his son. In 1943, they closed the business, the same year they wrote the valuation. Further close examination showed something was not right. The date of the valuation appeared to be two weeks after the official closure date itself, which was two weeks after the bombing. The obvious conclusion was that the valuation had been written and signed after the business had ceased to exist.

Of course, that didn't mean it was a forgery. There may be other explanations, such as the owner, or his son continuing the business from home. Next, David carried out a search of the deaths recorded in the St. James area of London, together with a census check. After some false leads, he came across an entry in the 1940 census, which listed William and Nora Baker living at an address in St James Park with a Mr Robert Baker aged 16, also resident. The names matched those on the company records.

Next, he entered the names and dates of birth of both men in the register of Births, Marriages, and Deaths. In 1973, William Baker's death was recorded, also at St James Park, but there was no record of Ro's death. However, there was a marriage entry in that name dated 1951; with a matching date of birth. A little digging brought up a brief newspaper article regarding the wedding. And a faded photograph of a man in uniform with his bride. The headline read, 'Local Hero Marries at St James Church'. The accompanying article read that Lt. Robert Baker and his fiancé were married at the church in a ceremony attended by friends and family. Lt. Baker was the recipient of the Distinguished Service Order (DSO) for his actions during the battle for Berlin in 1945. It took another hour of searching to find a current address. Knowing that Robert was likely the only person who could shed light on the mystery valuation, he wrote to him, care of the Union Jack Club in London. Now all he could do was wait.

....

For her part, Debbie returned to the ring's history. Using the notes David had taken, she zeroed in on the reference to the Titanic. There were 705 survivors of that disaster. Most were women and children, and many were rich. This was going to be extremely difficult and time-consuming. Then she noticed a snippet of information that may be relevant. One couple on the ship were famous and very rich, the owned Macys department store in New York, the Strauss's. Travelling back to New York, they had employed a new maid, a woman called Ellen Beattie. On a whim, she typed in the name and gold ring. Google came up trumps again; listing a reference to a radio interview with Titanic Survivor, Ellen Beattie, and a gold ring given her by millionaires, Ida Strauss. After 15 minutes, she found a copy of the interview for sale in a radio library. The cost was $9.99 for the CD. Not too much, though there was postage to pay from the US. Now the waiting began.

Meanwhile, Caroline De Winter was a troubled woman. Her interaction with Margaret and Ian had unwittingly opened the door into something far more significant. Whilst the curse on the ring had loomed large in the investigation, something else, something far more powerful, had emerged. Having passed the warning on to Debbie, she expected the spirit intrusions to abate, but the opposite was true. More and more spirits were trying to break into her innermost thoughts. It had been almost a month since she had taken part in any séance, and with good reason. A Medium has little control over which spirit contacts her, and they usually rely on the presence of a close family relative to do so. Now, however, the crescendo of voices had become too much. She knew she could not faithfully carry on charging for sessions that had no benefit to her clients. She had waived the fee for Margaret and Ian, after realising that this was no ordinary spirit contact. Like most mediums, she assisted troubled spirits in the belief that it would ensure her good standing.

At first, she suspected the lost souls were likely 9/11 victims who were desperate to contact relatives, but this theory just did not seem to hold water. The spirits were from another time period, all of them. She realised she could no longer ignore what was happening and deliberately channelled one of the most dominant spirits, a seaman from the 15th Century, who insisted on being heard.

Caroline switched off her mobile phone and took the land line receiver off its hook. For her own wellbeing, she had confided in another medium that she knew was the genuine article, and had invited him round. Philip Watson was co-incidentally also a police officer in the City of London Police, and had been a spiritualist for several years, a fact he did not openly broadcast. Though, as a police photographer, he was not in direct contact with the public.

It took Caroline about two minutes to fall into a trance. Philip watched as her eyes twitched and her lips moved, silently at first, then vocally.

"Who are you? You need to tell me. No, no, too much. Stop now. Calm down. I can hear you, now tell me slowly."

She shook her head.

"No, this is meaningless, tell me, what others, what?"

There was a pause, and suddenly De Winters eyes opened.

"My God, Oh My God, no, it cannot be, cannot be."

She closed her eyes, shook herself violently, and appeared to faint in the chair.

Philip rushed to her; she was still breathing but fast and laboured. He gently pattered her face, and after a few seconds she opened her eyes, taking a couple of minutes to re-orientate herself. Concerned, Philip quickly offered her a glass of water.

As she recovered, he found himself puzzled. He had not detected any spirits in the room while Caroline was in her trance. Something was wrong he thought, but could not fathom what.

After a few minutes later, with Caroline more lucid, he spoke to her.

"So, did you find out what's behind this unrest?"

Caroline stared at him with a seriousness he had not detected before.

"Oh yes, I found out, I wish to almighty god I hadn't. I do not know the answer yet, but I know where to find it."

....

Debbie glanced through the mail that had landed on the hall carpet. Just the usual bills and adverts, however one was different, a jiffy bag containing American stamps. The sender's name, The American Radio Archives and Museum. Quickly, she took all the mail into the Kitchen where David was finishing his breakfast. She handed him the envelope.

"I think this is the CD of the radio interview, you were waiting for."

David took the envelope and tore it open. Inside, was a compact disc with a label that read;

Interview, Mrs Ellen Beattie 61 yrs.

Newport Studios

Rhode Island

April 15th 1942.

David took out disc and loaded it into the player, and pressed play.

"We have a special guest on the program, Mrs Ellen Beattie. In 1912, Mrs Beattie was a passenger on the maiden voyage of the Liner RMS Titanic, which as we all know struck an iceberg and sank with a significant loss of life, in the North Atlantic. Now I understand, you were not a passenger as such, but were working as a maid for one

millionaire that was on the ship, Mr Isadora Strauss and his wife Ida. Is that so?"

"Well, not at first, I was actually in London, working as a maid and was happy in my job at the London hotel, when a guest approached me in the lobby; he was a very personable young man who introduced himself as Mr John Farthing. He asked if I had ever entertained the idea of travelling to America."

"Of course, a lady should not have really responded to this sort of question, but he was well spoken and seemed very educated. He informed me a Mr Isadora Strauss, a wealthy business executive who was looking for a new maid employed him. He and his wife had been in Europe for some weeks, trying to find a French maid for his wife. They had initially found an English girl who had left them promptly, as they were about to return to New York. He asked if I would consider the position. I felt flattered, and the offered salary was a significant increase compared to my current income. Whilst I was, to say the least, a little apprehensive about travelling abroad, I agreed to meet his employer."

Interviewer

"That would be Isadora Strauss and his wife, Ida?"

"That's right, we travelled to their hotel in a motorised hackney carriage. A wonderful contraption that didn't require horses and was propelled by a mechanical engine. I must confess it was a little daunting, but a wonderful experience."

"In line with their wealth, the older adults Strauss couple exuded elegance, with Mrs Strauss embodying the epitome of grace and politeness. On the way to the Hotel Mr Farthing had informed me that his employers owned a large store in New York, called Macys. I had heard tell of this store, and it was, in fact, quite famous. She asked me several questions, and these included my experience in service and my marital status. I feel they wished to ensure I had no husband or betrothed to concern them."

Interviewer

"So, you travelled to Southampton and joined the Titanic?"

"When they informed me that they had booked passage on the new liner RMS Titanic, from Southampton to New York, I could bear to contain myself. This ship was the talk of England. The biggest in the world, and was unsinkable. Only the very well off could purchase a ticket. So, of course, I was totally star struck. At that stage, I would most likely have worked for free to be on board."

Interviewer

"Now you were a first-class passenger as an employee of the Strauss'. That must have been truly an experience."

"Of course, but one had to know one's place in those days. I had duties with the family that prevented me from enjoying most of the entertainment on the ship. There were many very important passengers, including John Jacob Astor. He was a very rich American, but I confess, I had never heard of him before the sinking. I saw the Captain once; he was speaking to one of his officers on the deck while I was attending to Mrs Strauss. He was an impressive gentleman, with a fine white beard."

Interviewer

"Tell me about the night the Titanic went down."

There was a pause in the tape; David sensed the interviewee was gathering her thoughts before replying. He had seen the same reaction in countless other witness interviews he had conducted.

Then she continued

"It was heart-breaking, a ghastly sight, with so many people crying, and scared. As they put their loved ones in the boats, I saw men kissing their wives, crying themselves. They placed Mrs Strauss in a boat, but Mr Strauss declined to accompany her. He said he would not go until all the women were safe. Then she got out and said she would stay with him, as she always had. It was heartbreaking to see. Then she came up to me, and told me to take her place in the boat. I

wish I had the courage she had, but fear overcame me and I got in. She handed me several jewels and told me to keep them safe for her. But then she changed her mind and took them back, before giving me her coat. It was an expensive fur one. She assured me I would stay warm with the coat until we were allowed back on board. Then they lowered the lifeboat, and we all left the ship. I had a feeling that we wouldn't be allowed back on board because I noticed that the front of the ship was lower in the water than the back. There was a lot of screaming and crew members on the lifeboat rowed away."

Interviewer

"But you didn't give back all the jewels. Tell me about the ring."

"That was the odd thing I found the ring in the pocket of the coat. The ring must have got caught up in the bottom, or maybe it was in her pocket all the time. But I knew it was not right to keep it, so when we got to America, I tried to give it back with the coat to her daughter, but she would not accept it either. She said that her mother had given me the coat and I should keep it."

Interviewer

"And the ring?"

"She refused to take it back. She said nothing, other than she wished that it had gone down with the ship, and she never wanted to see it again. So I kept it."

Interviewer

"What was the ring like?"

"It was very pretty, gold I think, with 7 emeralds, it was probably worth a pretty penny."

Interviewer

"Did you ever think of selling it?"

"No, not really, it was special, a ring from the Titanic that had belonged to a very brave lady. I kept it right up to my marriage in 1914. But then Edward and I had a child, Gwendoline, we named her; we both agreed that she would get the ring on her 18th birthday,

but god had other plans. She died on September the 8th, 1917. Then I remembered what Sara Strauss Hess had said to me, that she never wanted to see the ring again. She seemed to blame her mother's death on the ring. Now with Gwendoline's passing, we thought it was time to get rid of it. Edward said we shouldn't tempt fate."

Interviewer

"So you sold it?"

"Well, Edward did, but he sent a letter to the Strauss' and told them of our loss, and asked if they knew anything about the rings past."

Interviewer

"Did she get a reply?"

"Not in writing, but one of her servants came round two or three days later. She said the ring was an old English one that had once belonged to a Queen of England, who had cursed it, and all who owned it. She said her employees were told this, but initially did not believe such things. They knew it was a fine piece, and a great example of early English craftsmanship."

Interviewer

"Pretty romantic stuff, did they say who the queen was?"

"No, they said she had met a sticky end and blamed the ring. Maybe her old man had her head chopped off. Like Henry, the eighth did to his wives. Anyway, that scared the owners, so they sold it to Mr Strauss. When they both died on the Titanic, the family just wanted rid of it."

Interviewer

"That's understandable. So what happened to the ring?"

"Edward sold it to a collector at a New York Historical Society event in New York, in 1920."

Interviewer

"Did he tell them the story of the curse?"

"Actually he did, but he said, as he had no proof or papers to prove the story, it did not add to the value. We were just glad to get rid of it."

Interviewer

"Well, thank you for sharing your story with us, Mrs Beattie."

The recording ended and David ejected it from the player. Debbie was the first to comment.

"Well, it gives us a little more information; now we need to find out the name of the collector."

David smiled

"Yep! That's the fly in the buttermilk, as our American cousins would say. Linking the ring from the Titanic to a bombed out shop in London is a pretty tall order. Fancy another coffee?"

Chapter 11

Ghosts from the deep

Three days after the tape had arrived, David got a phone call, from Robert Baker, informing him he would be happy to meet him over the next two days, as he was attending a regimental reunion of the Hampshire Regiment event in Aldershot, and would be free in the mornings. David quickly arranged the meeting, thankful that, as he was on leave, accepting such meetings was far easier. The venue chosen was the officers' mess, of Princess of Wales Royal Regiment, which now incorporated the Hampshire's. Baker's status as a WW2 hero had some influence, it seemed.

Baker started the conversation.

"Well, Mr Spencer, I must confess your letter came as a surprise, albeit a very welcome one. Normally, I am asked about my wartime service and supposed hero status. It brought back fond memories of my father and family before the war. So how can I help you?"

"Well, sir, I am researching an item of Jewellery that has recently come into my possession. I purchased it in as an anniversary present for my wife in Portsmouth, and am trying to find out more about its history. That investigation led me to you, or rather, your father, and the business you owned in London."

Baker nodded

"Baker and son, yes, the building was destroyed during the Blitz. I'm afraid all the records went up with it."

David produced a copy of the receipt and handed it to Baker, who pulled out a pair of glasses from his top pocket and scanned through it. His face darkened as he read it.

"You see, sir, there appears to be a discrepancy on the date, and I believe in the valuation."

Baker looked up

"You should be a detective, Mr Spencer."

David smiled.

"As a matter of fact, sir, I am. A DC with the Portsmouth police, but I assure you, this enquiry is nothing to do with my profession. The Statute of limitations has exceeded the limits for any crime that may, or may not, have been committed during the war. My interest is just to prove its history."

"Forgive me, but your father has grossly underestimated the value of this ring. I looked him up and he had a stellar reputation for straight dealing. I cannot believe he was just mistaken."

Baker looked up from the receipt. For a moment, he seemed unsure of how to react, and then looked up at David.

"No, it was not a mistake, Mr Spencer. I remember this item, a stunning Tudor period ring. The owner was a personal friend of my father, a woman named Ellen Beattie, and she specifically asked for a low valuation, actually she wanted a statement that it was not genuine, and a valuation to match that statement. I remember her name, because my father said she was a Titanic survivor. I thought that was unlikely, so I looked her up."

"He never discussed the reason she wanted a false valuation. He said it was personal. Had it been the other way round, a request for a higher value, he would have suspected something nefarious, and would not have done so, but this seemed to be different. She wanted someone, or some entity, to believe the ring was of no real value."

David nodded

"I must confess, that has baffled me too, but I don't suppose it is important. You have cleared up the key question; that this ring is the same one I bought for my wife. Would you happen to know its present value?"

Baker smiled

"Well, considerably more than the receipt shows, but I would need to examine it again to be more certain. It's been a long time since I saw it."

David unexpectedly produced a ring box from his coat and passed it to him.

"Well, I just brought it with me, in case you couldn't remember it too well."

Baker opened the box and took out the ring; he then produced a jeweller's eyepiece and inspected it.

"Well, it's certainly a fine piece, defiantly Tudor, and an exquisite example at that. In today's market, probably around 10 to 12 thousand pounds. Your wife is a very lucky woman."

He handed the ring back, and David returned it to his pocket.

"Well, she probably has your father to thank for that, if the seller had known its true value there is no way I could have afforded it. So, you have my gratitude, sir."

....

When Caroline De Winter called him, Geoffrey Hawthorne felt surprised, and her request took him by even more surprise. She wanted him to accompany her on a visit to Portsmouth Dockyard, to visit the Mary Rose wreck, currently displayed in a covered dry dock close to the preserved 19th century warship, HMS Victory, the flagship of Admiral Nelson, at the Battle of Trafalgar.

He had not spoken to her since the night of the Anniversary party. During the call, she had explained that it had become important to her to visit the wreck, but was concerned about how such a visit would affect her. The request was unusual, but in any case, Hawthorne agreed.

He agreed to meet her at his favourite café in Gunwharf Quays; and had spoken to his wife, and called Debbie to inform her, therefore avoiding any misunderstandings. He had promised to update her on the visit afterwards.

Prior to her visit, Hawthorne had done some research on the ship. When Caroline arrived, he informed her that although the ship was open for viewing; it was secured behind a screen, as they were continually spraying it with a wax preservative solution to aid conservation.

This did not provide a clear view of the wreck. The Mary Rose Trust had promised that they would end the spraying in about 5 years, allowing for the display of the ship with an unobstructed view.

Close by was another building, called Boathouse no 5, which was a temporary museum housing the artefacts, and a modern reconstructed section of the hull, showing a gun port. As they approached the building housing the wreck, Caroline felt the presence of many separate entities. At first, she could suppress these voices and noticed that they could not be described as menacing. Instead, they seemed like lost beings trying to find out where they were.

On entering the Building, this changed dramatically. She saw a sea of faces clearly in her mind, and all seemed focussed on reaching out to her. She faltered and took hold of Hawthorne's arm.

"Sorry, Geoffrey. I need to get some air."

She said hoarsely.

Geoffrey escorted her past the concerned-looking visitors and outside. For a moment, she sat on a low wall and took several deep breaths. She then looked up at him, her face a little flushed.

"I'm sorry. Geoffrey, that was a bit more traumatic than I had bargained for."

Geoffrey nodded, sensing her discomfort.

"Understandable. I sense you have achieved what you were looking for; do you feel like sharing it with me?"

Caroline did not look at him directly when she replied.

"When I got involved with this matter, I was sure it was all about a warning that a spirit wanted to deliver to your daughter. If that had been the case, with the message delivered, I would have expected a reduction in spirit contacts, but the opposite is the case. There was a compulsion for me to come here today, specifically to The Mary Rose. Until I got here, I did not know why. There is a great feeling of despair present here; I felt it as I approached the building, a strong feeling of anger and despair. Now I may have expected to feel some presence of the men who died here, but it was more than that. It is very difficult to explain."

Geoffrey did not really understand, but he knew that Caroline, who had a lot of experience in such matters, also could not explain it. He was concerned, not just for her, but also that his daughter may be in danger.

Caroline sensed his concern almost immediately and thwarted his impending question.

"I can see you are wondering about your daughter and son-in-law, well I do not sense any direct connection. I really think these spirits are feeling a great sense of injustice. No, not injustice, that's the wrong word. They have a sense of betrayal, a feeling that someone sacrificed them without cause or redress. One spirit, in particular, told me they are saying lies about us. It's all lies, because the truth cannot be told."

Geoffrey tried to make some sort of sense of that sentence before commenting.

"Are you suggesting that someone is lying about being on the ship or something else?"

"Not the ship, the history of the ship. The history is all wrong."

Caroline was now thinking hard, trying to rephrase what she thought. Finally, after at least a minute, she spoke.

"I think they are trying to tell me what actually happed, not the accepted history of what the Trust says happened. There seems to be a difference."

Geoffrey had picked up a guidebook in the entrance to the display building. Now he leafed through it until he found the section he was looking for; a history of the sinking. It stated the ship had inexplicably turned sharply, causing the vessel to list, which forced the open gun ports below the waterline, causing a large amount of sea water to enter the lower decks, and capsize the ship. He showed the text to Caroline.

"It sounds plausible enough to me. Have your spirits got another theory?"

Caroline was not amused and snapped back.

"They are not my spirits, Chief Inspector, or yours. They are those of long dead sailors, who are asking for a help I cannot supply."

....

David was not really looking forward to this session with Ruth. Although one could assert that the sessions were working, at least the dreams had subsided, he was still unsure of their value. The relationship with Debbie had really improved, and he put that down to the way they had both thrown themselves into research on the ring. He kept the appointment anyway. For her part, Ruth had planned to do some more preparation for the session, and the day before had consulted Professor Walker. The fixation David had seemed to centre on his belief that he really was the incarnation of a 15th century archer on the Mary Rose. She had to admit, although she had dealt with other cases of supposed re-incarnation, none had been this intense. Walker could not attend the session, because of a lecture he was giving on the same day in Manchester, however, had again asked for a copy of the recording of the session.

She began the interview as she had with the others, and spoken to him about the dreams, and had there been any developments. David will talk, but decided not to mention his, or Debbie's, contact with Caroline. He felt it would overcomplicate the matter, and was still considering the possibility that the whole spiritualist thing was purely psychosomatic. He did, however; mention the ring that they had both been researching. She seemed genuinely interested in the research undertaken, but David surmised correctly that she was just relaxing him before the hypnosis.

"Now, David, I want you to relax and clear your mind. As I count, I want you to remember things long past. We are going back to your schooldays, you are 7 years old today. It's your birthday. Do you remember?"

David's eyes remained closed, but he smiled faintly.

"I am 7 now, and mum has a party planned for me when I get home from school."

"And what did you get for your birthday?"

"Luke's light sabre, it's cool."

"Ah, Luke Skywalker's Jedi Weapon, yes that is really cool. Alright David, now we are going further back, back into the darkness, back to the Mary Rose, and Joan. It is the day of the enormous battle. The ship is about to leave. What do you see?"

For a moment, David did not reply. Then he began to speak. Again, the old Shakespearean dialect came through.

"Big crowd cum owt for ta see us go, twas a real sight ta beold. Grace Dieu is off our beam, all banners unfurled in the sunlight. Yes, tis a magnificent sight to beold. So many are ear lining the Wharf and quayside, the King was ere earlier, gave a speech on the Grace, but it was aboard Grace, too far to hear what he wuz sayn, but I sees him clear enough, Sir George was over there, with the other masters, but e's back aboard now."

Ruth now spoke quietly and clearly.

"Is the king still here? Can you see what he is wearing?"

David replied,

"Not now, e's gone to the Castle to watch the battle. He wuz wearing his black doublet, and a big gold chain, couldn't see much else cos of the crowd, but he was wheeled around in the tramme."

The remark puzzled Ruth, but decided not to interrupt, letting him continue, and safe knowing that the session was being recorded. She did, however, prompt him on another matter.

"Is Joan there, on the dock?"

"Yes, she were so afeared, so she was; said she, I must promise to take care. She gave me back the ring, said it would keep me safe, but a fighting ship is not a safe place for such a trinket. Can't trust some of these foreners. So I told her to keep it with her till I got back."

Without realising it, Ruth now switched to addressing him in his assumed identity.

"John, let's go forward an hour. Where are you now?"

"Off the Spit, I can see the Frog fleet now. Off the island seems to be 8 or nine ships so far. Tis a great day for battle. Tis said King Harry is at the castle watching us. We all cheered as we passed the castle, but couldn't see him. The gunners are ready, and we are cleared for action. The gun ports are now open and the guns set. We are holding course and headed straight for the lead ships. Looks as though we aim to cut-em in two, and give em a solid broadside as we pass. If we're in luck, we may get one each side. We are ready below with the boarding nets, can't see so good now, but the officer can. He'll give us the order as we pass in range. Looking hard through the netting, and I see the topsails of the frog ship. Waiting for the order. Make ready. Then the port side guns fire. We got the jump on the frog gunners. Such a noise, like the end of the world. Smoke is choking, can't see. Then we heard the officer shouting, 'LOOSE'. My first arrow is high, and I lost its flight, lost in the damn smoke. The others are all away. They are cutting a swirl through the smoke. I can hear the Frogs' screams as they struck. I can hear the Frog ship firing now. Not so many guns, we must ave spike a-many with our broadside. I can hear the Frogs screaming

and crying out, as more arrows skewer them. Not all ours. Some must be from the Grace."

David's description was vivid, and Ruth could clearly visualise the scene as the great ship surged through the waters of the Solent, exchanging fire. However, she kept probing, hoping for a sign that this was not an actual memory, but something conjured up in his turbulent mind.

"Is the French ship close? Can you describe her, and the people on board?"

David's reply was instantaneous.

"She's pulling astern of us. Can't see too clearly now with all the smoke, but we shot her up. She has no full working main sail. We need to come about. That's not good, the sky - tis weird, sort of shining, fading from the sun; no matter, low on arrows, twill take us around 10 minutes to come about, time enough to get more from the forward store. Joes running short too. Why is the sky so fearful? It's a bright summer's day, is it not? How can that be? No clouds on a sunny day. No wind, the sails are hanging loose, but all the other ships have sail? Tis a much confusing sight, so tis, right over the ship, now I feel the wind, an icy wind coming from above us, now why just us? It took the wind and turned it topsy-turvy, and we are not moving. The frogs will be upon us, sure as night is day. Time to get to the store, and the arrows, we'll need them shore as night."

There was another longer pause. Ruth looked up from her notepad.

"John, where are you now? What's happening?"

David's voice had now changed, and she detected genuine fear.

"It's got us. We are listing over, my God, it has us, the sea has us in a grip, there is no storm; the wind has us like an evil servant of Neptune."

Ruth tried to calm the rapidly rising tension, now apparent.

"What is it John that has you? Tell me, is it the cloud, what you can see?"

David's voice was now reaching panic overload, his eyes now open and darting around the room, but mainly staring at some imaginary horror above him.

"Tis no cloud. Tis a demon from hell, it is pushing us over, holding us over, Sir George is shouting from the upper deck, calling us all manner of cursed fools, water is coming in thro the gun ports. Got to get back on deck. The cannons have shifted; they have moved the ship further over. I can hear the screamins as the cannons roll down the deck; we've gone too far, she's going over. My God, water, so much water, that demon we're done for. Can't get back up the ladder, water is too strong. It took my arrows."

David's voice was now filled with panic and he began to cough and splutter.

Ruth quickly moved to end the session.

"David, stop, stop, relax, the water is gone, the ship is gone, we are coming back."

David continued to thrash around and became more violent. Ruth knew she had to break the session now, and fast. Such action could be dangerous. She knew you should never waken a patient from hypnosis suddenly, but she now felt there was little choice. She grabbed his collar and shook him hard, shouting, *"Wake up, wake up NOW!"*

David's eyes opened wide, and full of fear, his struggles subsided, and his breathing slowed.

"Dr Walters, Dr Walters, what are you doing here, what..?"

Now his eyes became focused, and he swiftly scanned the office.

"A Dream. It was just a stupid dream."

Ruth patted him gently on the arm.

"Yes, David, just a dream. Can you remember it?"

He looked at her with a more serious expression than she had previously witnessed, and whispered with conviction.

"Yes, Dr Walters, this time I can. A great ship, an old sailing ship, filled with water and trapped me below in a storeroom. I couldn't fight the water, and I was drowning. There was a storm over us. But not really a

storm, like a tornado, I think. The sky was clear, not dark, but the ship was being pushed over under the water. It was so real, so terrifying. I think this was the dream I've been having lately, but could never remember, but this time I could."

"Good, David, that's good. Do you remember the name of the Ship?"

"It was called The Rose."

Then the buzzer sounded on Ruth's desk, breaking her concentration, and David's. Her receptionist's voice came over the speaker.

"Dr Ruth; is everything alright. I heard shouting."

Ruth was on the point of snapping back but checked herself, realising the Receptionist was just concerned. She took a deep breath before replying.

"Yes Shirley, everything's fine. Thank you for your concern. Can you fix 2 coffees for Mr Spencer and I?"

She turned back to David, who now seemed quite composed, and then he commented.

"Good answer, Doctor, but I think we both know everything is far from all right."

....

The effect on Ruth had been almost as traumatic as it had been on David. After he had left, she cancelled her remaining appointments for the day, and called Professor Walker's number, leaving a message, asking him to call as soon as he returned from the Seminar. Try as she might, she simply could not dismiss this patient as merely suffering from hallucinations. Maybe the learned professor would have some answers. For his part, David had seriously considered telling Ruth about his and Debbie's encounters with Caroline, but again, decided against it. Probably it would not help, and would be more likely to complicate matters. Anyway, he felt he now had gained valuable information. Before he could not remember any details of the dreams, now it appeared he did, and with stark clarity, made as many notes as possible before the dream slipped from memory. He put this clearer memory down to him being awoken suddenly. After all, it made sense. Often, if some outside noise abruptly awakened him from a dream, he frequently had a clearer memory of the dream. This appeared to be a common psychological trait among most people he knew, including Debbie.

When he got home, he would tell her as much of the dream as he remembered. Maybe she could speak to her father, or even Caroline, about it.

While David had been reliving the horrors of the Mary Rose sinking, Debbie was making progress in tracing the ring's history. A check on the American Historical records threw up 3 potential collectors of Titanic Memorabilia, all were now deceased. There were two society events in 1920, only one was open to the public. Ironically, the society was able to supply a microfilm print of the handbill for the event.

It mentioned a showcase of shipwreck items, including a number from the Titanic, which included Lifejackets and personal items. It was a good bet that this was the event referred to by the Strauss's maid on the CD. Debbie, with a keen analytical mind, had prepared a family tree chart, tracing the ring back from her possession to the Strauss's possession aboard Titanic. The next step would likely be more tricky, establishing how the ring came into the Strauss's possession. Either they had bought it in Europe during their search for a new maid, or they brought it with them from New York. Debbie concluded the former, based on her family's insistence that they did not want it back and their belief that it was cursed. Unlikely if it had been a family heirloom.

Debbie had to admit, the evidence was thin and circumstantial, and it certainly would not reach the legal bar of proof. But this was no criminal investigation. With each passing decade, she could follow the ring's history and uncover another connection to the English Queen. She shut down the computer as she heard David's car pull up outside.

As he entered the house, Debbie immediately noticed the change in his demeanour. He went to the cocktail cabinet and poured himself a large Bacardi and coke, with rather less cola than normal.

Debbie went to him and gave him a peck on the cheek.

"*So, how did the session with your shrink go, sweetie?*" She already sensed the answer would not be fine. She was right. He looked at her with an almost far away vacant look that she had rarely seen before replying.

"*To be honest, it was pretty unnerving. The hypnosis triggered the nightmares again, though this time, I could clearly remember the dream. I remembered every detail. Now I'm convinced more than ever that this is not some mental short circuit in my brain. I know what I was doing when I died, and I know where and when it happened. I still don't know why this is coming back to haunt me now.*"

"*What does Ruth say?*"

David laughed, almost contemptuously.

"*I don't think she has a clue. The profession rejects, totally, the whole concept of reincarnation, so she is flapping around like a fish out of water. I cannot see the point of continuing these sessions. Can you, seriously?*"

Debbie took his hand and told him, forcefully, to look at her.

"*I think you need to talk to my father, and then to Caroline. You need to put aside your pre-conceived notions, and ideas, about the whole after life debate. Would it surprise you to know that Caroline is getting some unsettling dreams as well, all about the Mary Rose and its crew. Now, she does not know you, and never met you before the party. As far as I know, has never met Ruth either. Unless you believe Ruth is sharing confidential medical files with clairvoyants, and then you need to ask yourself, do I need to investigate this, even if it goes against my basic beliefs. If you find evidence that seems to show your suspect may be innocent, does that mean you should ignore it and put it in the bin?*"

Chapter 12

Answers

"Caroline, it's Debbie Spencer. I need your help. Can you call me back as soon as you get in?"

Debbie replaced the receiver and turned to her father.

"Well, Dad, hopefully she will call me back. It was difficult persuading David to agree to speak to her, but I cannot think of where else to go."

Geoffrey smiled at her and shook his head slightly before replying.

"I think you made the right call, but I cannot guarantee she will help. At our last meeting, she was pretty shook up and scared. She said this was a totally new and unnerving experience for her. Whether or not she agrees to help will depend on what's in it for her."

Debbie nodded, cynically

"You mean, how much can she charge us for her services?"

Geoffrey shook his head.

"No, that is not what I mean. I deem myself to be a pretty excellent judge of character; Caroline is not in her profession to make money. She sees it as a vocation, in the same way as you are not a police officer for the money. No, what I mean is that if she cracks this case and dispels the bad dreams, or as she would put it, banishes the evil spirits, then her reputation in the Psychic community would significantly improve. But if she fails, the damage caused to that same reputation would be immense. From her point of view, it's a gamble. But if it helps, one thing that Caroline and me have in common, along with you and David, is that we are all truth seekers."

Debbie looked up at him and noticed a change in her father's demeanour.

"You like Caroline, don't you Dad?"

Geoffrey looked up at her, choosing his words carefully.

"As a matter of fact, I do. She is a fascinating woman to talk to, and in some ways, reminds me of your mother."

His voice trailed off as he recalled some distinct memory.

Debbie took his hand.

"It's alright dad, I miss her too, but as you have often said, life will go on. It's been almost 4 years, and Caroline has made you smile again. That has to be a plus."

For her part, Caroline De Winter was still in shock over the revelations of her visit to The Mary Rose ship and museum. She had half expected that she may sense the spirits of the dead crew, however; she had put the possibility quite low. The Ship was not where it had been when they died. They moved the ship ashore and now it is under cover in a temporary storage facility built over a dry dock. Also, hardly 40% of the ship remained. The rest eroded away or still encased in mud on the sea bed. Although it was common for dead and restless spirits to remain at the scene of their demise, it was almost unheard of for them to follow a vehicle around after an accident. An exception was the case of the 'Ghost of Flight 401', a book by the same author that wrote 'The Airmen Who Would Not Die'. The filmmakers turned that book into a popular movie, and they manipulated many of the facts to enhance the storyline. Caroline's library contained both books. There were, however, some factual differences between that case and the Mary Rose spirits.

Both seemed to contain warnings, but the ghosts of '401' appeared in several aircraft that seemed to have no connection with each other. Later, it was reported that all the sightings were in aircraft that were flying with salvaged parts from flight '401'. The concerned airline never truly established or admitted this. However, some people later made unsubstantiated claims that all sightings stopped after removing the salvaged parts.

Caroline had reviewed the evidence of that case, but decided that commercial concerns had clouded the evidence presented by the airline concerned, and the exuberant film makers, to over dramatise the events. Therefore, we could not fully trust the evidence as presented. There was a common theme; both cases involved warnings from the other side, usually warnings of an impending disaster from an aircraft or ship. In David and Debbie's case; the warnings, if that is what they were, came from spirits who had died 500 years ago. What could they possibly be warning anyone about? However, the spirits had been very active, almost demanding, that they felt wronged, and were begging Caroline to free them.

Caroline had been mulling these things over in her head while doing research on a separate case. When she returned, she noticed the phone message indicator flashing. Playing Debbie's message back did little to lesson her unease. It was two hours later when she finally returned the call.

....

Ruth had spent many hours reviewing her last session with David and had not as yet shared the tape with Professor Walker. She had, however, been studying other documented cases of apparent regression to past lives. In an effort to bring forward some reason, she had been interested in the apparent randomness of these occurrences. There seemed to be no actual evidence that showed a person who died was immediately reborn as another human being. Most cases had gaps of around 100 years, although some, particularly in the Indian sub-continent, did detail children who swore they were the reincarnation of those who had recently passed. Some recently bereaved widowers had met some young girls, and insisted they were reincarnations of the wife they had recently lost. It was of course, impossible to separate these cases from religious beliefs, and this clouded the evidence, to a point it became, at best, unreliable.

Set against this was the undeniable fact that David had a clear and precise picture of the last moments of the Tudor warship, Mary Rose. His account did not exactly match the accepted historical facts on the sinking, though it would be fair to say they did not totally alter them. The Ship had sunk during a battle in a stretch of water called the Solent, between the south coast of England and the Isle of Wight. Contemporary accounts by both the French and English had given different reasons for the sinking. The French, understandably, claimed the heavy cannon from the French fire sank her.

Taken at face value, David's account graphically recreated the scene on board during the sinking. If David had studied the history of the sinking and the vast amount of information now available online, he could easily explain this. But he had no such interest in the ship, or its history. There seemed to be no reason for him to invent such a story; rather than assist his career, it was far more likely to end it. Finally, she made a copy of the tape and, somewhat reluctantly, mailed it to Professor Walker.

Meanwhile, Caroline had heard from Margaret Soper. In an email she had informed her she had experienced another dream involving the spirit named Joan. This had not been in any way threatening; in fact, it was almost benign. The Email ended with a question. Was it possible that the spirit was trying to reconnect with her for another reason? Temporarily postponing Debbie's request, she contacted Margaret via telephone. It transpired that the dream had been about a marriage, specifically Joan's wedding day. The dream was unclear about times and dates, but Margaret had played a role as an attendant, possibly as the matron of honour. Caroline considered that this may simply be a confusion of thoughts, possibly with Margaret thinking of marrying Ian and the Joan figure giving her blessing. However, there may be another explanation, a desire to pass information, to assist in unravelling the mystery. She returned to that theory after speaking to Debbie.

For the moment, what troubled her more was the malevolent entity that seemed to be present in the background. Whatever it was, it seemed to hold great power over both the living and the Spirit world.

....

Professor Walker had listened to the tape, sent to him by Ruth, twice now. So far, he had not acknowledged to Ruth he had even received it. No doubt that this was a very serious case, unlike any he had encountered before. The problem was that although his analytical mind flatly rejected the entire idea of reincarnation; he was struggling to find any other explanation. He also knew that Ruth was expecting him to find one, almost pleading with him to do so. There was another situation that was weighing deeply on his mind.

As well as being an eminent psychologist, the professor was also an enthusiastic historian, and had a degree in English History. He had once written an essay on the Reign of Henry VIII as part of his MA. After reviewing the recordings, he had done some revision. A distant memory had come to the fore involving a letter he had purchased a while ago, which mentioned a ring. He had not used the letter in any of his work, keeping it purely as a reference material. Now, he took the nicely framed letter, along with the modern English translation, out of its case in the bureau. He took the translation and sat down to read it carefully.

Sept 5th 1569.
Dear Emily,
It is with some trepidation that I write to you regarding the awful events that have

befallen our family, of which you must now be aware.

I believe my troubles first began with the ring that I inherited from my late mother, Joan Spencer. This was a jewel of great splendour, and was apparently made for King Henry Tudor, as a gift to his second wife, Mistress Anne, and it had been in my late mothers' possession since the time of his reign, though strangely she had always refused to wear it. This I understood, as it had been a gift from her first husband, and therefore it would have been unseemly for her to have exposed it to his male ego, you know how men are, My husband and I were desirous to give the ring to our daughter ,Isobel, upon her betrothal to Master Rushmore, whose business interests involved the Earl of Northumberland, Alas, these dealings made him many enemies who falsely accused him of plotting with the Earl in his attempt to depose her gracious majesty Elizabeth, Such accusations were of no merit, but it was to cause local supporters of the queen to assault their residence in Salisbury, and consign it to the flames, ending their lives and that of sweet Charlotte, who had yet to attain her 6th birthday. Isobel was wearing the ring on the night of her demise, and the magistrate, who deemed the fire to have been an unfortunate accident, returned it to me. My mother had often spoken of her belief that the ring was cursed, though in these times we do not fear such gossip. Now I fear that I may have brought evil upon this house.

Sincerely Yours,

Martha

The professor smiled to himself, as he remembered why he had bought the letter at an auction of historical documents some years ago.

The letter referred to the well-documented rift between Elizabeth 1st and her sister Mary Queen of Scots, which had ended tragically for the latter, who was beheaded in the Tower for plotting against Elizabeth. Of course, anyone of importance did not sign the letter, so it did not cost him too much. Now he wondered if there may be a connection between it, and Ruth's case. Of course, the names did not match exactly and there was no mention of either the Mary Rose, or a description of the ring. However, it was intriguing.

Despite having agreed to meet with Caroline, David still had his misgivings. He knew of several officers on the force who ardently believed in both life after death, and reincarnation. He also knew that the same officers were, while not exactly ridiculed, were branded as dreamers who were not quite in the same world as everyone else. He had invited her round to their home, primarily to avoid being seen with her outside. Since the anniversary party, many of his friends now knew who she was, Both Debbie and David had referred to her as a friend of Debbie's father, when asked; and to date, and that had been enough to squash the rumours. David looked up as the gold Mercedes pulled onto the drive outside. After a warning to David, to ditch his sceptical attitudes, she went to the front door.

She greeted her guest warmly, and David rose from his chair as Caroline entered, and extended his hand.

"Nice of you to come, Mrs De Winter, I know you must be very busy."

She took David's hand with a genuine smile, which froze momentarily as a surge of unseen energy hit her through his hand.

"Well, we all have priorities in our lives, David, but I feel your experiences are at the top. Debbie has told me of your last session with your hypnotherapist. Would I be right in saying, that she could not fully explain your dreams?"

David grinned as he replied.

"I think that would be an understatement Mrs De Winter, her receptionist almost called the police."

Seeing the alarm on Debbie's face, he quickly added.

"Ok, perhaps that is a bit of an exaggeration, but it certainly alarmed her."

The last comment acted as a bit of an icebreaker, as Debbie's father had said that Caroline De Winter was an amiable person to talk to.

"As you surmised, my hypnotherapist seems at a loss to explain these premonitions, and dreams. However, until now, I couldn't remember any of the details of them, nor too much of the sessions under hypnosis. That changed, when Ruth, my hypnotherapist, woke me suddenly after becoming concerned for my welfare. Now I have a clearer recollection, but it still is a mystery."

Caroline replied

"So, you're asking, why me; why do these spirits choose my life to disrupt?"

"Exactly; I have no connection with any of this."

"Well, it's a good question; I think it concerns you, because you have latent memories of your life aboard the Mary Rose. What has triggered these memories now? Most often they occur in childhood, but fade as one gets older. Just occasionally, they come sharply into focus in adulthood. Often, the reason is unclear, but there is always a reason. In your case, I think it involves something, or more accurately, someone outside the Ship or its crew."

David seemed suddenly very interested.

"You mean like an evil spirt, or a force that is overpowering and terrifying?"

Caroline nodded

"That's exactly what I mean; did you experience such a force while under hypnosis?"

David's voice grew quieter.

"It was like a great storm, exerting great pressure from above, forcing the ship down, and over on its side. There were no clouds, no waves, or anything like that. It was as if a giant hand had reached down and grabbed the ship, holding it down as the water flowed in. Like when you

are pushing a jug down in a sink full of water. For a moment it still has buoyancy, then as the water fills it, it overcomes that and slowly sinks."

There was a pause, then Debbie spoke.

"Not that he would know that, based on his lack of washing up experience."

If the light-hearted remark was supposed to lighten the conversation, then it failed miserably, though Caroline displayed a slight smile.

"Did you remember anything else about the voyage before you sailed?"

David shot a glance at Debbie before replying.

"Bits, flashes really, but I remember giving a ring back to someone, Joan, I think. She had asked me to take it for good luck, and I told her it would do that better by staying with her to keep it safe. Funny that the ring looked like the one I bought for Debbie. Somehow that episode got implanted in the dream. Weird how that happens in dreams, reality and fantasy mixing. Ruth said it is common in dreams."

Caroline nodded

"I agree with her, but not in this case. I think you are remembering the incident clearer than you are letting on, most likely to avoid a negative response from Debbie. I believe the ring did not just look like the one you bought her, it is the same ring, you gave back to your wife in 1545 on the dockside at Portsmouth, The Hard. Only that wife was not Debbie, she died over 400 years ago."

"Fair Joan"

David almost whispered the name. Then he looked back at Caroline.

"How, I mean, how could you know that?"

He sat back in the chair, still trying to make some sense of something that was completely nonsensical. Caroline tried to elaborate.

"I believe that all of us have lived many other lives before this one. After we die, and are reborn as someone else, we lose the original conscience

of what we once were; think of it like buying a good quality, but second hand computer. You do not want, or need, the previous owner's data, so you reformat the hard drive, erasing it, and leaving you a blank canvas, so to speak. However, sometimes, if you have the right codes, you can still recover fragments of the old data, correct?"

David did and replied,

"You mean like the police do to recover child porn, or bank details, or just deleted data as part of an investigation?"

"Correct. Well , mediums like myself can sometimes recover the passwords that enable us to do just that. In your case, someone wanted to warn you about the ring, however, that was only half of the equation. You see, this ring has come up before in the dreams of the two other clients I have that do not seem to have any connection with you. You've been given the message, which should have ended the entire problem, but it didn't. I am still trying to find out why?"

Debbie now joined the conversation.

"Well, I don't know if it helps, but David and I have been researching the ring. We have traced it back from the dealer David bought it from to 1912. One victim, Mrs Ida Strauss, a millionaire who died with her husband that night, gave it to a survivor of the Titanic. The survivor was her maid. We know this, because she did a radio interview some years later, and we got a copy of the tape on CD. David apparently revealed more under hypnosis, but cannot recall the details. Ruth would have the tapes, but I doubt we can get access to them. She would consider them confidential."

Caroline was suddenly very interested in this revelation.

"So, have you asked her if you can hear the tapes yourself?"

David nodded

"Yes, I have, more than once, but she said she would not want to do that at this time, as it may cloud the sessions and make treatment more difficult. I may force her to hand them over legally, but not without garnering unwanted publicity for myself."

Caroline nodded

"Alright, David, can you remember anything more about Joan, from your last session, say where you lived, or if you had any children?"

David knew Debbie would hang on to every word, so chose his words carefully, trying to give honest answers without annoying Debbie. He hoped he would be as understanding if the roles were reversed.

"I remember her talking to me on the quayside. She was frightened, but she was trying hard not to show it. She was wearing the white shawl around her shoulders, the same one she wore when I met her. Not sure about children, there were none there with us, so maybe not. Weird, this woman Joan was supposedly my wife, but I honestly cannot remember anything about our life, where we lived, or any friends. I am sure we were married and more than just friends."

Debbie had been listening and now joined the conversation.

"Joan was the name he called out in his sleep during the nightmares. It was also the name he called out when he was a child, or so his parents told my father. That is why I did not think he was having an affair. That bit of information may just have saved your life, honey."

She added with a wink.

Caroline also smiled before continuing.

"Yes, that I surmised, the memories of previous lives are clearer in the young, because they are usually fresher. But that does not really explain this one, unless John Grainger was your immediate past life."

David, who was still trying to get his head around having one previous existence, which was bad enough, but the contemplation that there may be many more, was unthinkable at this moment. He asked anyway.

"Is that really possible?"

"To be honest, I do not know. I have not heard of it before, but I suppose it is theoretically possible. Yes!"

Debbie shook her head

"Damn, that's scary."

There was a moment's awkward silence that was broken by an incoming phone call on David's phone. He looked down at the screen before whispering,

"That's good timing."

"David Spencer."

The female voice on the other end answered.

"Hello Mr Spencer, Dr Walters's receptionist. Dr Walters would like to speak to you, if it's convenient?"

David replied and then put his finger to his lips to show they should keep quiet. Then he pressed the speaker button.

"Hello David, hope I am not interrupting anything. I wanted to ask you what you felt about our last appointment. I hope you have suffered no ill effects, or any more nightmares."

Aware that Caroline was now listening, he replied, trying not to sound nervous.

"No, not really, but I recall the details of the dream clearly now, for the first time. Now I understand my recollections were bizarre, but I suspect the previous tapes were none the less so."

"I think you really should let me hear them. I understand your reasons for being reluctant to do so, but I think you agree and those reasons are now moot. Anyway, I will conduct the research into this 15th century ship myself. And I think it would help me if I could compare the factual history with my dreams, would you not agree?"

Ruth replied almost instantly.

"As a matter of fact, I do, and for the very reasons you suggest, which is why I am calling you. I have made copies of the tapes and will leave them with my receptionist for you. She has instructions to only hand them to you personally, and I must ask you to be prepared to sign for them. Is that OK?"

David confirmed it was OK and thanked Ruth before hanging up.

Chapter 13

Confronting the evil within

Professor Walker had not done anything regarding the letter he had rediscovered, but it had been preying on his mind for some time now.

Finally, he did a little research. Taking the translation from its case, he placed it open on the desk with his laptop. First, he looked up the Earl of Northumberland, who the letter showed was involved in a plot against Queen Elizabeth the First. Then he added the name Rushmore. He meticulously followed the links until he got a hit; Martin Rushmore, who was the owner of a trading schooner that ferried goods between the port of Southampton, and Calais. He died in a house fire outside Winchester, on September 1st, 1569. This was 5 days before the letter. Good, but not proof; he needed more. Further searches on the names Joan Grainger, and Joan Spencer, did not turn up anything of value, until he switched the search criteria to census and parish records.

Then he zeroed in on a marriage report dated July 6, 1550, between Robert Spencer of Christchurch, in Hampshire, and Widow Mrs Joan Grainger, of Poole, in Dorset. Again, not conclusive, but very strong evidence that Joan had remarried in 1550 and had at least one daughter named Martha, and a granddaughter named Isobel, age 19 when she perished in a fire along with her fiancée, and their infant daughter.

The Professor sat back into his chair. Michael Walker, the historian, and Michael Walker, the psychology professor, had a conflict when they realized that David Spencer may have a direct connection to their family. Now he had to decide whether to pursue this ancestry, or file it away under the, 'don't go there' heading in his mind. A lesser man would likely have done just that, but there was of course, a simple, but slightly cowardly alternative. Later that afternoon he called Dr Walters.

....

Caroline De Winters had a well-appointed flat. It overlooked the River Thames, and the newly constructed Eye, Ferris wheel about a mile downriver. Margaret scanned the external keypad and pressed the button marked 'De Winter C'. After a few seconds, Caroline answered, and then signalled to unlock the door. In Central London, such security precautions were essential for all residents living and working in the city. Caroline met her at the elevator on the 4th floor.

Margaret spoke first.

"*Thank you, Mrs De Winter, for agreeing to see me. I am not too sure if it is even relevant. The Dream was not disturbing, but I was worried it may mean something that I am unaware of.*"

Caroline immediately put her at ease.

"*No, really, it is I who should apologise to you, for not getting in touch sooner. As a matter of fact, I have been involved in the same investigation that concerns the spirit, Joan. So I am keenly interested in what you recall about the dream.*"

Margaret relaxed a little and began.

"*Like I said on the phone, it was a little bizarre. The dream was of a wedding between the woman Joan, and a man who I did not know. It was old-fashioned, Elizabethan I think, judging by the clothes the guests were wearing. When I woke up, I made some quick notes, as you do after a dream. I brought them with me.*"

She opened her handbag and produced an envelope containing several folded pages. After scanning them, she continued.

"*After the service, I overheard a woman talking to Joan, telling her she looked great, and how pleased everyone was she had finally found happiness. I do not clearly remember her husband; he was a fairly tall man with a well-trimmed beard. Several friends surrounded him. I remember thinking; he should be with his new wife. The thing is, I cannot recall why*"

I was at the wedding. Few people spoke to me, so far as I can recall. That did not seem strange in the dream, but I realised it was odd when I woke up."

Caroline thought for a moment before responding.

"Did anything wake you up?"

Margaret looked up in surprise.

"Well, as a matter of fact, yes, but how did you know that, ESP I suppose."

Caroline chuckled

"Love to say yes to that, but in truth, most subjects only clearly recall dreams if an external force awakens them suddenly. So what was it?"

"Fear, a sudden chill of fear, don't know what it was, but I got an overwhelming sense of relief when I awoke, Like I was being chased, and had got back in my house, and safety; or at least something like that. I wrote the word werewolf, in my notes, but in all honesty, I don't know why."

Caroline had also been making notes, and responded abstractly, without looking up.

"It's called Cognition Processing, the attempt to rationalise, irrational thoughts. It's pretty common in dreams. The brains amygdala generated this, very relevant in the thought processes that are active in REM sleep. Oh, sorry, please go on."

Margaret seemed surprised.

"You sound like my University Professor, Michael Walker, he's always going on about that stuff, but he would never consider it in any way connected to reincarnation. That would be unscientific."

Caroline perked up at Margaret's comments. During their meeting with David and Debbie, earlier, he had mention Dr Walker being present at one of their hypnotherapy sessions. She had therefore done a little research on him prior to this meeting with Margaret.

"Actually, I have heard of Professor Walker. He is eminent in the field of parapsychology. And I understand, has an MA in History. It would

indeed be interesting to compare notes with him on this case, though I cannot ever foresee him agreeing. There would be ethical problems regarding client confidentiality, on both sides. However, both sides also have to understand the workings of the human mind to a degree. The problems arise with the interpretations of those workings. The plain fact is that neither side is prepared to concede the other may be right."

Margaret agreed and ventured

"Doesn't that ever really frustrate you, Mrs De Winter, I know it does me?"

Caroline laughed before replying

"Constantly, now let's get back to your dream; I want you to concentrate on this fear you felt that woke you. You mentioned it was akin to being chased by a werewolf?"

Margaret shook her head,

"Well, maybe not a werewolf as depicted in the cinema, more a presence of the danger one would feel, if confronted by such a creature; if you follow me. You know the feeling you get when walking alone, especially at night, when you think someone, or something is following you, you keep looking behind you, and that increases your fear. Well, it was sort of like that."

Caroline understood the analogy.

"The spirit world exists between two plains, the living one we all inhabit now, and the one yet to come, our future life, if you like. Some people, myself included, are privileged. No, that's not the word. Maybe cursed is better. To be allowed access to that world, usually when a spirit is restless or has an important message to convey. However, as in our world, there appear to be other spirits, dark spirts, evil, if you will, that oppose this contact, see it as a threat. It is usually those spirits that interrupt communications, a little like political opponents who constantly interrupt each other in debates."

"I must admit, that is not my idea of what heaven would be like."

Margaret's response seemed to almost express disappointment. And it brought a faint smile to Caroline's lips.

"Well, heaven is really a question of faith, all religions have it. The ancient Vikings called it Valhalla, the Hindus, and Buddhists, Nirvana, Native Americans, the Happy Hunting Grounds; all describe it as a peaceful place that awaits us all at the end of days, a hope or desire of better things to come. I must confess; I am worried about this intrusive spirit, though. I have decided to try to channel him again, direct."

Margaret was concerned, and it showed.

"Won't that be dangerous? He sounds like a powerful entity to me?"

The reply was less than reassuring.

"It will be perilous, that's a fact, but I have a friend who is also a medium. He could intervene if necessary. I feel somehow, this spirit is the key to this total mystery."

....

Caroline had taken no chances with this séance. She had already prepared the room and set up the recording, and other equipment, plus a video camera to record any manifestations that may become visible. It was 11 AM when Phillip arrived. Immediately, he sensed Caroline's apprehension. This was a gamble, but Caroline felt she had to do it.

She closed her eyes, and Phillip started the recording. At first, not much happened. Caroline was becoming fidgety, as if searching for something deep in her mind. The thermometer fluctuated, and the room air pressure rose, but not dramatically. These were finely calibrated instruments, with over 100 times the sensitivity of a standard household barometer and thermometer combination. It was an indication that there was a disturbance developing.

Caroline then spoke.

"I know you are near. I can feel your presence. What do you want from the land of the living?"

There was no response. After about 30 seconds she spoke again, this time more forcibly.

"What's wrong little man? You are scared. I feel it, scared to reveal yourself. Are you so weak?"

This time she got a response, a male voice deep and in an almost Shakespearian dialect.

"Be silent, you worthless wretch, you dare to address me; after you have seen my power in both my world and yours."

There was no sign of Caroline being intimidated. She snapped back.

"You have no power over the living. You may scare them with your dreams, but you can do nothing to me or the people who now have the ring. It's over, begone, now."

Phillip saw a surge in the energy levels, and a vapour cloud appearing in the room. He could just make out a surreal, indistinct shape in the cloud. An Elizabethan figure of a man with his fist clenched. The sight was alarming, but Phillip knew there were no recorded cases of a spirit harming a living person, at least not directly. Now Caroline seemed to have an argument, but he could no longer hear the male voice.

"Not true. You have no control over the ring."

"No, not now."

"That's pure fantasy. If you have a point, make it. You're wasting my time."

"Tell me, did Anne really bug you so much?"

"What? Considering you killed the queen, can you hardly be surprised? What did you expect?"

"Really, well do you worst kiddo; I'm getting bored listening to your pompous ego."

Phillip noticed the readings were all returning to zero. Caroline opened her eyes, and for a moment said nothing. Then she saw Phillip.

"Did you get anything Phil?"

She asked almost casually, but it was a ruse. Phillip could see Caroline was anything but calm.

"*We got something, but you will have to fill in the blanks. As the last debate was one-sided, I could not hear him.*"

Caroline took a deep breath and sat back in the chair.

"*I know. He blocked you. Somehow he sensed the recording gear, but he made it plain he would stop me from investigating. He didn't say how, so I need to be careful.*"

After about 10 minutes, Caroline played back the video recording. It clearly showed the materialising cloud, and with the aid of the pause/stop feature, they could see the outlined figure. It was not clear enough to recognise features, but Phillip had a stab, anyway.

"*Looks a bit like old Henry himself to me. Is that possible?*"

Caroline looked again at the image.

"*Do you know, that was my first suspicion, someone used to having his own way, and who wielded great power, but this man is not the king, he is someone far more dangerous, someone who kills without compulsion, just on a whim.*"

Phillip Smiled at her.

"*I know you, Caroline De Winter; you know who it is, don't you?*"

Caroline nodded; this was frustrating for Phillip, who followed up.

"*So, are you going to tell me, or what?*"

Caroline shook her head.

"*Not yet, it's too dangerous, believe me Phillip, you don't want this man in your head.*"

It was past 6 when Phillip left Caroline's flat. It had been a pretty tiring day, and she took a shower before turning in. However, she could not sleep well. She finally turned on her bedside lamp and picked up the paperback that had been on her bedside cabinet for over a month. Tonight she felt she may finally finish it. After half an hour, she felt sleepy enough to give it another try. Downstairs, in the flat below, a retired civil servant in her 60s had also retired for the night. After boiling a pan of milk for her customary mug of Horlicks, made up the beverage, and put the pan back on the burner, before taking the drink and going into her bedroom after switching of the kitchen light, she failed however to notice the faint glow from the ring under the pan.

Two hours later, the automatic smoke detectors sounded, and the Local Fire Station received a flash call. They made the scene in less than 5 minutes, by which time the top of the building was well alight. Some survivors were streaming out of the building, and police were cordoning off the area.

Chapter 14

Death reaches out from the other side

Margaret's meeting with Caroline had really inspired her, and with Ian's help, she began a file, listing the mounting evidence of a case of reincarnation that she actually had a walk in part. She swotted up on the information known about the Mary Rose and the crew. Over 400 had perished when the ship sank. About half the crew had remained entombed in the hull. The forensic team carefully removed the skeletons for analysis. From these examinations, the occupations of the recovered remains could be determined. The forensic team carefully analysed the skeletons and determined that most of them were archers. They identified at least 5 individuals with a muscular build and stature near one of the big guns, suggesting that they were gun crew. They found the remains of a ship's dog, along with crates stacked with longbows and arrows. It built up a tragic picture of the disaster. Her research had also put a human face on the episode. These were not just skeletons buried in mud. They were once living and breathing human beings, who had loved, enjoyed life, and had families who grieved at their loss. Possibly one of these skeletons was John Grainger, married to fair Joan. All this made Margaret more determined than ever to discover all she could. Hopefully, Caroline could help. For now, she had a lecture to attend from Professor Walker. She definitely could not be late for that. She shoved the file in her duffle bag and scurried out to the lecture hall.

About half an hour after the class had dispersed, Professor Walker realised he had left his cell phone in the lecture hall and returned to retrieve it. As he strolled past the desks in the empty room, he spotted

138

the folder on the floor. Margaret had accidentally dropped it from her bag when leaving. He picked it up, intending to place it on his podium, but then noticed the heading; 'Case of David Spencer, by Margaret Soper', curious, he opened the folder. The header page read; 'Thoughts on past life regression from the Tudor period'. Now the file really caught his attention.

Instead of placing it on the podium, he had hung onto it. Margaret's next class was due the day after tomorrow, which he knew would give him time to study the notes before returning them.

Meanwhile, Margaret realised the folder was missing and carried out a cursory search of her room. After failing to find it, she Called Ian.

His reply was not what she wanted to hear.

"Sorry, the last time I saw it was when you were in Professor Walker's class and dropped your bag. I noticed it fell out, and you quickly put it back on your desk, and put your bag on top. I assumed to hide it from Walker. Is it possible you left it there?"

Margret thought back

Damn, I heard something drop when I picked the bag up at the end of the lecture. I could see nothing on the desk, but it may well have fallen under it. I hope Walker doesn't find it.

Ian's reply was reassuring.

"Oh, he didn't. I saw him leaving while you and the others were packing up. We need to get to Wednesday's session a little early, and find it before anyone spots it. What was in it, anyway?"

Margaret's face showed her mood.

"It was everything about the dreams, and the séance with Caroline, not to mention her contact with the Spencers; that was confidential stuff. I hope to hell I can get it back. In future I'll keep that stuff under lock and key."

Meanwhile, unbeknown to both of them, Professor Walker began reading Margaret's notes; quickly he realised they referred to the case of the same David Spencer, who Ruth Walters was treating. As far as he could tell, the two had not met, and even if they had, he was sure Ruth would not discuss a patient with a mere student. As he read on, more information cemented together. Ruth's notes, and those of this mysterious medium, Caroline De Winter, had created a complete picture of David's past life regression that fit the facts perfectly, but defied all scientific and medical theories.

He knew Margaret Soper was a young, and intelligent student with an enquiring mind; he actually had read her book, though had not yet disclosed that to her. Now he found it difficult to counter her conclusions on the subject. However, this file had given him the opportunity to talk to her privately about her research and possibly help his protégée, Ruth Walker.

The lecture proceeded with no sign that the Professor had read, or even found, the missing file. He took questions from several students on certain aspects of the human psyche and summed up the subject with his recommendations for further study. As the class dispersed, however, he approached her.

"Ah, Miss Soper, how are your studies going into your past life regression theories?"

At that moment, she realised that not only had the Professor found the file, but had almost certainly read it.

She swallowed hard before replying.

"Actually, sir, I am a little puzzled by some of the contradictory theories. It's a little frustrating."

Walker laughed and smiled before replying.

"Welcome to the world of scientific research, Miss Soper. It is always, if never, frustrating."

He tapped her lightly on the shoulder, producing a smile of relief.

"If you are free after supper tonight, I would relish the opportunity to discuss it further with you, in a more private setting, say the 'School Study' if you are able."

Margaret, had in fact, planned to spend the evening with Ian, off campus; but this was far more important.

She replied

"Sir, I would feel honoured. What time do you suggest?"

Walker glanced at his watch.

"Say 7 PM."

As he left, Margaret hurried to Ian, who had been waiting discreetly at the back of the hall.

"Well?"

He enquired

"Has he got the file?"

Margret smiled smugly to herself before answering.

"Oh, he's got it, and probably read it too; he wants to discuss it after supper in the study room. And I'm going to; in fact, wild horses wouldn't keep me away. Sorry about this evening, but there will be other times. This is very important to me."

Ian replied

"Yes, I can see it is. Well, if the school hasn't thrown you out, I'll see you tomorrow."

He kissed her lightly on the forehead and was gone.

Margaret walked into the study room, which was, as expected, all but deserted. She was around 10 minutes early, but Professor Walker was already there, seated in an armchair, one of 3 around a small table. She walked over to him and sat down, noticing her file was lying on the table.

"Good evening Miss Soper, please have a seat. First, I wish to return this to you; I found it on the floor close to your desk after the previous lesson."

He picked up the file and handed it to her, adding;

"You should really take care of your research notes a little better. Losing them usually entails the loss of many hours of study."

He smiled as he added,

"Ask me how I know."

"Thank you, sir. I will remember that. Did you actually read any of the file?"

Margaret was hoping he would say no, but it was, of course, a forlorn hope.

"Actually, I read all of it, not because I was being nosey, but because your subject is actually a patient of mine, or more accurately, a colleague of mine who sought my consul on the case. From your notes, I see you based your prognosis on paranormal séances with a medium from London, and conversations with David's wife. Is that so?"

"Not quite, Professor. I have actually never met Debbie Spencer, though Mrs De Winter has, and I only found that out while she was assisting me in a vivid dream I had been having regarding a spirit called Joan. Whilst describing her to Mrs De Winter, she seemed troubled."

"Troubled, in what way?"

"Well, she said that she felt there was something not right with a spirit trying to contact me directly, said it was unusual. My boyfriend and I invited her to visit us in the Cotswolds' for a private séance to discover more."

"I see, and how much did Mrs De Winter charge you for this service, if I may ask?"

Margaret smiled, sensing the Professor's scepticism immediately.

"Actually, she charged nothing, we offered, but she said it was not a money issue; she wanted to help me if she could."

Margaret's answer seemed to surprise Walker, who thought for a moment before responding.

"Well, that is unusual; anyway, what did this séance reveal?"

"Well, it's in my notes, but she told me through Joan's spirit that someone called Debbie was in danger from a ring that David had bought her, and we had to warn her. The voice was unique from Mrs De Winter's normal voice; it had a deep West Country accent, and sounded, well, less refined. I learned through her that David and Debbie were police officers. Actually, she said watchmen, but Caroline said that was a medieval term for the police. She said that Debbie must be warned and sounded terrified. She also blamed the ring on the death of her husband, John, who had drowned because of it. Then, as the séance ended, Mrs De Winter's voice came back, her own voice this time angry and aggressive. Then it changed again into a male voice, angry and threatening to destroy her. It was weird, Caroline shouted back and her normal voice returned. I wrote in my notes after she left. It appeared Caroline had won the argument, but she said later, it was only the beginning. An evil spirit intruding in the séance, and offering threats; I know this sounds pretty wacky, but it seemed to stop my dreams, at least until this week when I had another concerning a wedding, involving the same, Joan, character. That bit is not in my notes; I haven't had the chance to update them yet."

Professor Walker said nothing for a few minutes, but picked up the file again and glance through it. Finally he put it back on the table *and* said;

"Extraordinary, totally extraordinary. It may surprise you to know I do not find any of this at all wacky, as you so aptly put it. But returning your file was not the only reason I wanted to speak to you. I would like to enlist your help. I want to show you something, a letter from my collection of Tudor manuscripts that I purchased some years ago. This is the modern Translation. He handed her two pieces of folded A4 paper.

"Read it and tell me what you think."

Margaret took the papers and read the contents slowly before responding.

"It's uncanny. Is this the same Joan we have been talking about? Who was so scared of the ring?"

The professor nodded.

"I believe it is, or at least may be. Now, I would be most interested in meeting with Mrs De Winter, but to assure her of my intentions, I would like you to give this translation to her, as shall we say, a token of faith. Do you recall, I mentioned a quotation from Shakespeare a while back when we spoke about reincarnation?"

Margaret did.

"'There are more things in heaven and earth than are dreamt of in your philosophy'. Yes, I do, Professor. In fact, I have ordered a t-shirt with the quotation on it. I feel it aptly describes the science of psychology overall."

Walker laughed at the remark before replying.

"Let no one persuade you to a particular point of view, my dear. Not even me. Do your research, check, and by all means, listen to advice from friends and your teachers. But in the long run, 'unto thy own self be true', Hamlet again, Act 1, scene 3."

He rose to leave and extended his hand.

"Well, good luck Miss Soper. I'll see you in class. I really hope Mrs De Winter will accept my invitation."

Margaret watched him go. She had learned something new about the science of psychology and the world of the Paranormal. It didn't seem like they were so far apart now, and if Professor Walker was an example of current thinking, maybe they could indeed build bridges.

....

The fire was now well under control. Outside, a ragged group of survivors huddled together, covered in blankets, while paramedics took care of them. Philip approached a police officer.

Could you provide information on the number of fatalities and injuries?"

The Officer turned to him, and upon recognising him, replied.

"Just the one death as far as we know, sir. Don't know the injuries yet. Your friend was very fortunate."

Caroline smiled

"He has a habit of turning up when needed."

She kissed him lightly on the cheek before adding,

"Just don't tell your wife." Before walking back to the car.

Phillip joined her; when they were out of earshot, she whispered to him.

"The lady who died was a neighbour in the flat below. She did not deserve to die, it was me that should be dead. Mrs Halliday was just collateral damage."

"Yes, I kind of deduced that. So where will you stay tonight? Jean and I have a spare bed."

Caroline shook her head.

"Thanks for the offer, but I'll check into a motel for a few days while the insurance sorts things out. Luckily, I backed up most of my work on my thumb drives, which I keep in the car. I was thinking of upgrading my desktop, anyway. Hopefully, the insurance money will enable me to do that. Every cloud has a silver lining, so they say. By the way, why did you come back tonight?"

Realisation came over his face, and he glanced back at the building.

"Damn, my phone. I had left it in your flat and it's still there. When I smelt the smoke, I completely forgot."

Caroline smiled

"Well, fortunately for me you did, and fortunately for you too, look what I have in my bag. I spotted it before turning in."

At that moment, wife, or no wife, he could easily have kissed her; he smiled as he took the phone. Caroline started the engine and pulled away. He switched on the phone and dialled the number.

"Hi Darling, it's me. I'm on the way home, and tonight I could really do with a hug."

Chapter 15

Off the Radar

Margaret saw the report of the fire at Caroline's flat in the London Evening Standard, and immediately tried to phone her, the number was no longer in service. The part of the building containing Caroline's flat had been extensively damaged, as shown in the picture in the Standard. The article stated that there had been one fatality, a retired parliamentary secretary named, Edith Halliday. Eight persons were still undergoing treatment. She was on the verge of checking out the hospitals, when Ian suggested she try emailing her, Margaret could not believe she had not thought of that, and quickly did so. In the Email, she related her conversation with Professor Walker and stated his wish to meet her, and that he had produced a letter, written in the 15th Century that seemed to shed some light on the Spencer case. After an agonizing wait of almost 3 hours, the phone rang.

Caroline explained that since the fire, she had taken precautions and changed her number, while she was safe and unharmed, she did not want to publicise her address. Simple precautions, but she felt prudent in the circumstances. She had also suspended conducting private séances for the time being. She offered to send a friend to collect the letter, but reluctantly, Margaret refused.

"Professor Walker was insistent that I hand it to you personally, I think he was worried that it may end up at a student frat house of something."

That was something she could appreciate. They agreed to meet at a café in the shadow of the London eye.

Margaret felt surprised when she arrived at the café and saw that Caroline was not alone. Phillip was with her; both seemed pleased to see her. Without delay, Margaret handed over the letter.

"This is a copy of the letters translation. Professor Walker said you are welcome to visit him at the school and examine the original."

Caroline took the letter and read its contents.

Margaret waited for her to finish before speaking.

"I feel I may have misjudged the Professor. He did not take issue with me on my research as I expected. If it counts for anything, I believe he is trying to help."

Caroline nodded and passed the letter to Phillip. After he read it he passed it back.

"Your thoughts, Phil?"

"Well, it seems as if the letter, assuming it's genuine, and adds credence to the investigations so far. I am intrigued why he has shared it with us."

"Well, I will have to ask him that when we meet."

....

At the same time as Caroline was agreeing to meet Professor Walker in London, David had collected the tapes from Ruth, and had taken them back home. Aware that Caroline had expressed an interest in them, David played them first, with just him and Debbie present. But on the spur of the moment, Debbie had suggested her father join them. He arrived about half an hour later, and with some trepidation, David started the cassette player.

People made brief comment for the first two tapes, and then as David prepared the third one, Debbie spoke up.

"This is pretty haunting stuff, Honey; are you really saying that you believe this?"

David just shrugged

"I don't say that, how can I, this is the first time I've heard my voice under hypnosis, it's different from listening to interview tapes. I do not remember saying this, but it stirs flashes of memory. To be honest, I'm not sure what to believe. What do you think Geoffrey?"

Aware that both eyes were now on him, he answered definitively.

"I think we are all a bit out of our depth on this, we need a second opinion from someone who is an expert in this field."

Debbie nodded

"Caroline De Winter,"

She said almost reluctantly.

"Quite so,"

He replied

"I tried to call her today, but her number is no longer active. Odd that."

David quipped

"Maybe she didn't pay her bill."

An attempt to lift spirits but no one was laughing, least of all Geoffrey, who had already checked her out, and found she was far from hard up. She owned her flat outright, and her Mercedes was only a year old.

....

"Sorry to intrude Professor, there is a Mrs Caroline De Winter at reception who wishes to see you. She states it is of a private matter."

Michael Walker put aside the papers he was reading and looked up.

"Oh, yes, Mrs De Winter, I was expecting her, can you escort her to my office, I'll be there directly."

He glanced at the study clock; it read 12:55 PM. This woman was punctual. He had suggested a meeting between 1 and 3 PM, when he had a break from lectures. That was certainly a point in her favour.

First impressions were good. Caroline's attire was well put together and she communicated effectively. He asked her to sit down and opened up the conversation.

"Thank you for accepting my invitation, Mrs De Winter. I have heard much about you from mutual acquaintances who speak highly of you. Although I cannot agree totally with your hypothesis on the theory of reincarnation, I hope I am not too biased to reject it out of hand. I do really believe that we both are trying to help this young couple. And that can never be a bad thing."

Caroline took his hand warmly.

"On that, Professor, we can most certainly agree. I am glad you reached out to me, but also a little surprised, refreshingly so though, surprised. To be truthful, I am not used to dealing with cases so ancient. Usually, people come to me seeking reassurance of the spirit world, looking for my guarantee that their recently passed loved ones are happy, and will see them again. Sometimes, however, that is not always possible. The Spirits are selective and are not always cooperative. Rarely, they intrude with a stark warning; I believe this is such a case."

Walker nodded

"If you are right, and I'm not saying you are, then what is your interpretation of the warning, and why would a 16th century spirit have any reason to warn a 21st century police officer of anything?"

Caroline nodded thoughtfully

"It is certainly a conundrum, and that's a fact. It seems to be something to do with this ring. While there is a historical background, I'm unable to locate concrete evidence of its presence in written documentation. But there again, that may not be so strange. In itself, the ring is of little significance. So what do you think?"

Professor Walker nodded in agreement.

"It was the ring that first caught my attention. A student of mine, Margaret Soper, whom I believe you know, has been doing some private research on the paranormal. She is not alone in that. I have always

*encouraged my students to think for themselves, and not accept anything
as irrefutable. I became involved in this whole matter through a research
folder she inadvertently left in class after one of my lectures. Normally,
I would simply have returned it to her with no fuss. However, this file
was no normal theory. It concerned a patient of a colleague of mine, Dr
Ruth Walters, who has a practice in Portsmouth. She had consulted me on
David's case, and therefore I was familiar with the facts. Obviously, Miss
Soper could not have been. Yet the story in both the file, and my notes, all
but matched. That triggered my memory of the letter I had bought some
years back. The one I sent you the translation of. In anticipation that you
may want to see the original, I have brought it with me, together with a
photocopy."*

He opened his briefcase and handed her the framed letter. On the
reverse of the frame was a certificate of authenticity. Caroline studied
the letter for a few minutes, frequently comparing it with the
photocopy and the translation. Finally she handed the letter back to
Walker, who returned it to his case.

Caroline looked at the Professor. His face did not betray any
emotion as she commented.

*"Well, I must admit, this is pretty interesting evidence, and will help
in following the ring's trail. I know David and Debbie have been working
on the same trail, trying to trace the ring back from today. I believe they
have already done so, as far as 1912. As a history project, it is fascinating,
but to me, it may be also the key to the entire mystery. There are, however,
questions. One is that in the 1940s a jeweller intentionally gave a false
valuation of the ring. This was how David could buy it so cheaply. I am
curious, though, why that occurred. David was told by the son of the
jeweller concerned, that it was a private matter, and could not, or would
not, elaborate. That may have been the end of the matter, but David got
another communication from the jeweller's son this week."*

*"Apparently his father had been engaged to the owner prior to her
marriage, and turned to him for help when he was insisting she sell the*

ring, which was reputedly worth thousands, if it had really been Anne Boleyn's. Basically, she exploited his feelings for her to get him to declare the ring a fake, which allowed her to keep the ring. He only discovered this after looking through his father's personal journal, following David's initial approach. Personally, I am moderately convinced that the ring did once belong to Queen Anne Boleyn. There is still, of course, much more research to establish that, if we can, then maybe we can find why its effect has caused so much upset in the lives of this young couple."

Walker listened without interruption. In doing so; he could study Caroline's manner and sincerity. His reply was a little unexpected.

"Well, I may shed some further light on the ring's history. Since linking it to this letter, I have been carrying out my research. King's Collage has some interesting archives pertaining to the Tudor period. The author of the letter was Martha Spencer, the daughter of Joan Grainger, who had remarried in 1550, and took the name of her new husband, Spencer. Records confirm the fire story, and the dates match. Joan died in 1567 of the plague. Martha and a son, Jeffery Spencer, who became a captain in Drake's navy, survived her. In case it should come up, I would advise not to give details of Joan's death to David. It may cause, shall we say, complications; for the record, Dr Walters agrees."

Caroline replied

"I can see that, yes."

Walker continued,

"There is no further reference to the ring until Martha's death in 1589. Following that, I discovered a record of Sir Jeffry Spencer marrying a woman called Elizabeth Bishop. No lesser dignitary than by Sir Francis Drake attended the ceremony. According to reports, Spencer presented his bride with a fabulous gold and emerald ring that had belonged to his mother. Again, no proof it was the same ring, but it likely would be, unless he had somehow come about two, of the same design."

He now had Caroline's full interest.

"And do we know what happened to the ring after the marriage?"

Walker's reply was less than she had hoped.

"No, not so far, anyway. Elizabeth died in childbirth the following year, so I assume it reverted to her husband. I suppose, if you had been around, you may have seen that as evidence of the curse."

Caroline seemed far away as she replied.

"Something like that."

The Professor missed the clue hidden in her oblique answer, and continued.

"You strike me as an intelligent woman, Mrs De Winter. Surely you do not see evil behind every mishap. Are there not just unfortunate episodes that just occur at unfortunate times?"

Caroline smiled.

"You mean accidents will happen, well that's true, but I also give credence to the notion that most accidents have a cause. With this ring, I think the trail of accidents is so frequent that they all have a common cause."

Walker smiled, a trace of resignation etched in his face.

"The curse?"

"No professor, not a curse, which is just humanity's way of explaining ill fortune, and it has cost many an innocent life. No, I mean evil, an evil that has followed this ring throughout its journey. This week, it moved against me, and I take that very personal."

Walker raised his eyebrows at that remark.

"What happened this week?"

Caroline continued; her voice almost emotionless.

"A fire that was supposed to kill me, it would have done so too, had it not been for a friend who returned that evening to pick up his mobile phone that he had left behind earlier. I had been getting under the skin of this spirit, if that is possible."

She smiled at the idea of a spirit having skin, but continued.

"The spirit warned me earlier that day, but stupidly, I felt he could not harm me direct whilst in the spirit world. It seemed I was wrong."

"I think I read about that fire, in Savoy Place, well at least you were not harm"

Caroline's reply had a determination in it.

"Unfortunately, my neighbour below was not so lucky. Unwillingly, I had given the spirit an opportunity to strike me from the other side. In a way, I feel responsible for her death. Whilst I do not expect you to believe me in this, I felt you should be aware. I strongly believe this spirit poses a threat to not only me, but all who are investigating the phenomenon, that, of course, would include you professor."

....

Geoffrey Hawthorne was a little surprised to get a call from Caroline. True enough, he had been thinking about her since the episode at the Dockyard. She said she was in town for a meeting, and asked if she could meet him, as she had some new information. To the retired chief inspector, this did not ring exactly true, especially when he asked if she wanted him to pick her up, and was told she had her car and would come round. The 85 mile drive from London would take around an hour and forty-five minutes, and her Mercedes was not that economical on fuel. The train would be cheaper, and certainly a lot less stressful, especially if she was really on business, and on expenses.

At 2:30 PM, Caroline's Mercedes pulled up outside, and Geoffrey greeted her at the door. It did not take long for her offer the first surprise.

"Well, Geoffrey, I have a little confession to make, I am in Portsmouth purely to see you, there is no business meeting. The reason for the subterfuge was simply, after our last meeting I was unsure if you would agree to see me direct."

Geoffrey just smiled.

"That would be an incorrect assumption Caroline, I am always pleased to see you, my daughter said you have made me smile again, and

there may be some truth in that. So, what was it you said about some new information?"

"Well, two things actually, first, I had a meeting with Professor Michael Walker, he is a senior lecturer at Kings College in the city, and heads the Psychology dept. He had some information about the ring and its history."

Geoffrey found the news surprising.

"I've heard of Sir Michael Walker, David met him at one of his sessions with Dr Walters. Frankly, I am surprised he agreed to a meeting. I do not think he gives much credence to the world of the supernatural."

"He doesn't, but he is too smart a man to ignore the undeniable. You see, he has a student who has been researching your son's case, in a purely private capacity. He got to see her notes by accident, and he realised that her case, and the one involving your son, were the same. He spoke to her, whereupon she mentioned me."

Geoffrey was now becoming concerned.

"So, are you saying the professor, or maybe Doctor Walters leaked my son's case notes to this student?"

Caroline shook her head.

"That was my first thought, but it made little sense. I think Walker suspected me at first, but he then did something unexpected, he sent me a copy and a translation of an original 16th century letter he had bought a few years back, concerning a tragic episode involving a fire, and a cursed ring. After doing some research, he is convinced that the ring in David's dreams is the same one. He has also identified the writer as the daughter of Joan Grainger, whose husband died on the Mary Rose. So far, his research has traced the ring up to the early 17th Century. I have brought copies of the letter, translation, and Professor Walker's research to date."

She handed over the papers, and Geoffrey put on his reading glasses and read them carefully. For Geoffrey, the disclosure, especially from no lesser person than the highly regarded Professor Walker, was powerful evidence that the psychic world and the academic world had clashed. And traditional academic thinking was losing. After reading, and rereading, the letters and papers, he finally looked up.

"Well Caroline, if this was a criminal case; I would say these papers contain a prima face case of proof of the existence of the human soul surviving after death. How else can one explain these memories and facts being recalled under hypnosis, or in a séance? Does Professor Walker have any other explanation?"

"Well, he said that there are, as yet, unexplainable areas of human consciousness, such as telepathy, or sixth sense, but to quote that old warrior, The Duke of Wellington, I feel he knows how to defend a hopeless position."

Geoffrey looked up at her,

"Like some politicians I could mention. Well, I am flattered, but did you really drive here from your comfortable flat in London, just to bring me these?"

The smile on his face brought a similar reaction to Caroline's.

"Well to be honest, no, I just had to get away. My comfortable flat is gone, destroyed in a fire that should have claimed my life, and would have, if a fellow medium had not come back to collect something he had left behind. There is a strong, and evil, presence dogging me at the moment. So I needed to pass this stuff on, and to be really frank, I needed a sounding board, and you Geoffrey Hawthorne are an excellent listener."

Geoffrey was now looking at Caroline, not as an interesting medium, but as a mature, and possibly vulnerable woman. For him, his next question was a bit of a leap.

"So, I take it you are in Portsmouth for a few days, if so, would you do me the honour of dining with me this evening, as my way of thanking you for your help?"

Caroline looked up at him, almost coyly.

"Well, it's a long time since anyone asked me out on a date. Let me consider it. These decisions need to be weighed carefully."

She immediately laughed and continued.

"I would be delighted to, Geoffrey."

Her smile brought a great relief to him.

"Well, shall we say 7:30? I can pick you up if you give me your hotel."

She shook her head.

"No, I'd rather not give the hotel address. I may be safer that way, but I can come back tonight, and we can go from here."

After she left, Geoffrey called his daughter, informed her about having additional information that could assist her research on the ring, and requested her to come over.

Debbie had compiled a database on the computer, and was slowly filling in the blanks, it looked like a family tree missing most of its leaves, but now Geoffrey may add a few more.

Correspondence with the Strauss family had yielded that the ring was part of Ida's personal jewellery, and she had it with her when she left America. Thus eliminating the possibility she purchased it in Europe. According to the family's attorneys, it was acquired in the mid-1850s after being exhibited at the Great Exhibition in London. The display by a Jeweller in London sparked considerable interest, leading to the apparent sale of the ring to an American Army officer. David had unearthed a drawing of both the ring, and the buyer, a tall bearded military man who emanated from the state of South Carolina, named James Longstreet.

David recognised the name, and a quick crosscheck showed that Confederate General James Longstreet and the purchaser of the ring in London appeared to be the same. Next, David began searching for any connection between Longstreet and the Strauss family in New York. At first, there seemed to be no connection. The Strauss were born in Germany and Bavaria, respectively. But Isadora immigrated to the US in 1854. That meant they could have met just after the Great Exhibition. It was a long shot, and Debbie was still working on establishing a connection when Geoffrey arrived, curtailing her search.

Debbie now entered the new information into the computer tree and become more fired up, as the puzzle was now becoming clearer. At least for now, the history trail of the ring had supplanted the danger possession of the ring posed.

For Geoffrey, though, that same history also showed a disturbing pattern; one of death and hardship. Regardless, it was good to see his daughter and son-in-law working together, and as a result, watching the tensions ease between them.

....

Chapter 16

Opposites Attract

Inspired by her visit from Caroline, Margaret Soper may have hoped the dreams would have ended. It was a forlorn hope. That night, the spirit of Joan reappeared in another dream that caused her to awaken suddenly; an icy feeling of dark menace had engulfed her body while laying quietly as her eyes scanned the room. She was alone, and for the first time, felt extremely vulnerable. She could not clearly recall the dream she had just experienced. The memory, like so many before, jumbled and faded from her mind as the sunlight overcame the room's blinds, brightening the scene. She grabbed a pad and scribbled down what she could remember. By the time she had fixed her coffee, the memories were all but gone. She scanned the notes she had made.

*A dark wood

*The Joan figure, urging her to follow

*Ian, shouting at her, calling her a stupid bitch *Driving through the countryside, of her childhood *Faster and faster, the car seeming to have a mind

of its own

*Being unable to steer

She put down the pad and shook her head. Maybe Caroline may make some sense of it, she mused.

That would come later. Now she had a call to make and was unsure of how Ian would react. Anyway, she couldn't address it over the phone. She called him and asked to meet him at lunch in St James Park, simply saying that she needed to discuss something very personal with him, and away from the campus grounds. As usual, Ian was right on time.

Margaret kissed him lightly on the cheek and picked a secluded bench. Ian turned to her.

"*So, what is this serious matter that's on your mind?*"

For a moment, Margaret did not reply. She studied the ground in front of the bench as she tried to find the right words. Then she looked up at him. He could see the fear in her eyes.

"*Well, I know this is probably an about face in this world, but I want to suggest we live together, we share so much, and to be frank, I feel safer when you are with me.*"

Ian smiled. The same thought had been occupying his mind, but he sensed for different reasons. He took her hand and noticed a slight tremble.

"*So what brought this on? I mean, I think it is a good idea, but has something happened?*"

Margaret nodded.

"*Another bad dream, a scary one, not sure what it was about, but I woke up feeling scared and alone. I needed someone. In fact, I needed you, but you weren't there. Then I realised how much you really mean to me. I just do not want to spend any more nights alone.*"

Ian could see the tears in her eyes. He kissed her on the lips gently before replying.

"*I cannot think of anyone I'd rather wake up next to in the morning.*"

....

Geoffrey made his excuses and left after an hour, saying he had to prepare for an evening out with a friend. He diplomatically brushed aside questions from his daughter, which naturally caused her to firmly believe the guest was a female.

David resumed his investigation into the ring's history and stumbled onto an important clue. Isadora Strauss was a confederate sympathiser, and had been prevented from going to West Point by the outbreak of the civil war in 1861. They appointed him as an officer in a confederate unit, but due to his youth, they did not call him to active service. He did however; spend time in England procuring ships for the confederate blockade runners. A vital part of the Confederate war effort. The link between Longstreet and Strauss was now narrowing.

He continued to search on both google and Wikipedia sites for any connection. Both had survived the war, and lived early into the 20th century. Strauss had become a member of the US Congress, and in 1896, he became the joint owner of the Macys department store.

Longstreet however, did not fare so lucky, in 1862 an epidemic of scarlet fever hit the family, taking 3 of his children, 3-year-old Mary Ann, 4-year-old James, and 6-year-old Augustus. His 14-year-old son, Garland, also caught the virus, but miraculously survived. The effect was devastating on the family, and affected them all deeply. To David, this could well have been the reason he may have sought to rid himself of an unlucky, and possibly, cursed Ring. The trail of tragedy was unmistakable.

However, it was still pure conjecture. He sent another email to the Strauss's attorneys, thanking them for their help to date, and asking if the family had any record of the purchase of a valuable ring from James Longstreet.

The Montparnasse restaurant on Palmerston road Southsea was secluded and came highly recommended. Geoffrey had booked a table for 7:30 PM. He had chosen this place, because it was unlikely to be frequented by those who may know him, and did not want the dinner interrupted by over curious friends asking for introductions. Also, it was under new management, and he was eager to see how that had altered it. Once seated and having ordered, Geoffrey opened the conversation.

"So, tell me about Caroline De Winter, not the medium, the woman."

Caroline shrugged.

"Well, not much to tell really, you probably know most of it from the police record checks, and don't say you have done none, or I can call a cab right now."

Her smile was infectious Geoffrey grinned.

"No, I don't mean what's in the files, I mean the real Caroline. What for instance, do you enjoy for entertainment, TV, and cinemas?"

Now he felt awkward, and it showed.

Caroline helped him out,

"You're not very good at this small talk stuff, are you Geoff?"

Her smile betrayed a hint of teasing.

"To be honest, Caroline, no, I'm terribly out of practice, sorry."

He replied.

She reached across the table and touched his hand.

"To be honest also, Geoff, so am I, and I would add, I am pleased you're not one of those lady-killer Romeos who think they're so smooth. Believe me, I've met a few.

Ok, let's give you the rundown; I'm 46 years old, divorced 7 years now. My ex was both very well off, and a bastard who liked to show me off at society functions. One afternoon I caught him in bed with his attorney, a girl who was understandably eager to avoid a scandal that may affect her law career. When I filed for divorce, she advised him to make a deal, in return for not naming her as co-respondent. I got the house, and a generous settlement. I have no children, and before you ask, I am not seeing anyone at the moment, though there is a certain ex police inspector that has caught my interest. I think that's about it."

She raised her glass, still smiling.

Now Geoffrey knew why he liked her so much, she was bright, attractive, and fiercely independent. He raised his own glass to meet hers.

"Tell me Caroline, do you ever think of the effects of your revelations from the other side, what they may have on people on this side? I suppose what I'm trying to say is, and probably not very well; is do you ever think

some things are best left kept secret? Not in this particular scenario, but overall?"

At first she did not answer. It was a fair question that had often occurred to her. Finally she replied.

"Of course, that often occurs to me, in the same way as I'm sure it does to you. Say, for instance, you discover an unfortunate fact that bears no direct relevance to the case, but will deeply affect the family, or domestic relationships. In my case, something like a major disaster, such as 9/11, rarely throws up such conflicts, but this one is different. The Mary Rose sinking was centuries ago. It should not affect the present day world that it does."

Geoffrey nodded in agreement.

"Well, I suppose, in our modern world we can now view disasters in glorious colour and CGI on the big screen, and that brings such disasters to home. Films like Titanic expose the cost of human life. I wonder if such vivid portrayals may affect us in our sleep or dreams. Have you ever wondered if people like David or Margaret could relive such events in their dreams?"

Of course, Caroline had definitely considered that, in her conversations with Professor Walker, the subject had come up more than once. She lay her cards on the table, and judge Geoffrey's response.

"As a matter of fact, Geoffrey, I have I spoken about it with Professor Walker. It's true that things we experience in our daily lives affect us while we sleep. Children may get a nightmare if they view a film, or play a computer game, that is unsuitable for them. Some adults also experience such a blurring between dream and reality. But I believe that is only a partial answer. In this case, I honestly believe there is something more, something beyond outside influences. In terms of marine archaeology, including the Mary Rose, David lacks interest. Outside of his fishing interests, he has no connection to the sea either. Margaret, likewise, is from a totally different background, and although she has experienced an interest in life after death, a concept that first brought her into contact with

me, it is unprecedented that she would have the same dreams as David. Even Professor Walker could not explain that. Then of course, there is the sense of menace, and evil, experienced by both myself, and apparently, by David. Quite simply, there is a powerful force, or forces, at work here. It seems to be centred around The Mary Rose and this ring."

Geoffrey had paid close attention. He was unsure what Caroline was driving at, but decided not to put his concerns as directly by saying so.

"Are you of the opinion that the ring is cursed?"

"Carolin,"

Caroline leant back in her chair before replying, noticing that a staff member was approaching the table, and she enquired if everything was satisfactory, and then left when receiving that assurance. The interlude had given her time to frame her answer.

"Actually, Geoffrey, that's a conundrum; if you say, do I think people who have handled the ring believe it cursed, well the answer is straightforward. If you are asking if the ring has some latent power to cause evil or misfortune, then that is trickier. It brings on a deeper question: do inanimate objects have the capacity to retain forces and feelings. Metal, for instance, can magnetise itself, and exposure to an isotope can cause many objects to become radioactive. Some suggest that thoughts and ideas could be electrically generated and retained as latent radiation."

Geoffrey shook his head.

"I'm kind of sorry I asked."

He said with a smile.

"Well, what have you been doing with the time since the fire?"

Caroline was happy to get off the idiosyncrasies of curses and human ideas. She opened her palmtop device and read off the screen.

"Well, actually, I have been doing some more research on the ring's history. Particularly on Sir Jeffery Spencer. He was a captain in Drake's navy and the last contact we had for the ring. After his wife's death, historical records show he spent three more years serving at sea before being

appointed to a position in Elizabeth I's cabinet. He eventually remarried a duchess. He died in 1664. No direct mention of a ring, but they had a daughter. A girl named Emily. I checked on the registry of births and marriages, and came up with a record of a marriage between Emily Spencer, the only daughter of Sir Jeffery Spencer, and a man named Walter Harding. Recorded in 1642, he held the rank of colonel in Charles 1st's Royalist army. There is a mention of a gold and emerald ring being part of Emily's dowry. Again, no clear description. The battle of Naseby claimed the life of Colonel Harding in 1645."

She closed the device.

"Impressive. So what's the chance of us making the final links?"

By now, Caroline had realised another couple seated at an adjoining table. Particularly, that the male diner was not only interested in them, but his partner seemed to be speaking about them as well. Betrayed by her frequent glances in their direction, finally she spoke.

"Geoff, do you know that couple to our left, and slightly behind us. They seem to be pretty interested in us?"

Geoffrey replied without looking round.

"Yes, unfortunately I do. Before Winchester CID was restructured, I remember seeing Morton. He used to be a detective inspector. We were colleagues on many investigations. I had hoped he would not recognise me, but I suppose that was a forlorn hope. I really wanted to avoid such contacts tonight."

Caroline smiled again.

"You are a well know man in this town, Geoffrey. It's a safe bet people would recognise you. It's no problem, and don't worry, I can be very discreet."

Morton took advantage of a trip by his guest to the restroom to approach their table.

"Geoff, great to see you again. How you been keeping?"

The greeting seemed warm enough, and Geoffrey responded in kind.

"Enjoying my retirement. Oh! And may I introduce Mrs Caroline De Winter, a friend of mine."

Caroline smiled and took the offered hand with a nod.

....

Debbie's curiosity was nagging at her mind. She knew something had happened to her father. His whole demeanour had changed; she guessed the reason was a new woman in his life, but the obvious candidate, Caroline De Winter, was in London. So this could not be her. Maybe they had spoken on the phone, or he had planned to visit her in London. But that was crazy; he would not have left in the early evening to drive to London. David, of course, was of no real help. He simply said that she should leave the matter, and if her father wanted to tell her something, then he would. Until then, she should let the matter lie. Though he knew Debbie, and there was a fat chance of that happening.

Finally, he shut down the computer.

"Look sweetheart, I know that this thing with your dad is on your mind, but is that the only thing worrying you. You seem a little edgy."

Debbie had been waiting for an opportunity to speak to him and this seemed the right time.

"Well, if you must know, it's the ring. It's a wonderful piece of Jewellery, and it has a great provenance. In fact, it's that provenance that worries me a little. Now I don't give a lot of credence to this curse business, but Caroline does. I am sure she is holding back more than she is telling me. You, Caroline, and this Margaret girl, all seem intent on warning me, and they did so before you even bought the ring. That's why I haven't worn it. I don't want to tempt fate. In a way, I wish you hadn't bought it. I know that sounds goofy."

David put his arm around her.

"Not to me, it doesn't. In fact, I wished I hadn't bought it either. Maybe we should just sell it quickly and get you something else?"

Debbie now looked up at him with tears in her eyes.

"We can't sell it David. What if it's cursed, and its new owner dies? How would that make me, or for that matter, you feel?"

When the phone rang, it shattered the growing gloomy atmosphere.

When David answered, the caller surprised him.

"Hello, David Spencer, this is Sir Michael Walker. I apologise for calling you out of the blue, but I am trying to contact Mrs Caroline De Winter. She left London after a meeting with me, and seems to have dropped off the radar, so to speak. I know from my meeting with her she was doing some research on your case, and wondered if you had heard from her."

"Well, no, as a matter of fact, we thought she was still in London. I tried calling her, but she has changed her number. Because of a fire in her flat last week, she's reducing her activities. One of my students, who knows her well, thought she may be in Portsmouth."

Once she realised who was on the phone, Debbie showed an interest. She promptly forgot about the ring as David continued the conversation.

"Can I ask why you want to speak to her, professor, in case she should turn up? It is possible she may contact my father-in-law, who knows her well."

If he had been hoping for a clue, he felt let down.

"Well, if you should see her, tell her to call me. I have some more information regarding research I am doing with her. She'll understand."

Debbie had been close enough to hear the second part of the conversation and was now convinced she knew who her father's mysterious visitor was. She picked up the phone.

"I'm calling dad right now, to ask him."

David took the phone from her hand and placed it back on the receiver.

"Not a good idea, Deb. If you are right, then at this moment, him, and Caroline are out on a date. And he will not thank you for interrupting them. If you are wrong, it will sound like you are butting into his personal life. In either case, you will not be the most popular daughter in Pompeii."

Although she would never admit it, Debbie knew he was right; David sympathised and offered a solution.

"Look Deb, you now have a reason to call him, so call him in the morning, and tell him we got a call from Professor Walker, who is trying to contact her regarding some research. Tell him about the fire, and see if he has heard from her."

Debbie looked up at him with some alarm.

"Fire? What fire? Where?"

David sat back in the chair with a sigh; he knew he should have asked more questions.

"Apparently, Caroline's flat caught fire last week, and she had to move out while they renovate it. As far as I'm aware, she's okay, but she hasn't shared a new address or phone number. But what I want to know is what this new information is about and does it concern me and this damn cursed ring?"

....

Chapter 17

Dark Forces

The Royal Naval dockyard at Portsmouth Hard was a busy and popular location, and was the premier tourist attraction in the City. It housed the famous warship, HMS Victory, Lord Nelson's flagship at the Battle of Trafalgar, - HMS Warrior a mid-19th century ship, fully restored - and now, of course, the partial remains of King Henty VIII's flagship, the Mary Rose. However, after the gates closed, and the tourists had gone, it was a far bleaker place. Naval personnel carried out regular patrols, and security was tight. Since the attacks on the world Trade Centre, Britain was taking no chances. Warrior and Victory both maintained night security personnel. The museum staff locked up the Mary Rose building along with the museum. Both had alarm systems.

At around 2 AM, the space alarm inside the museum activated and sent a message to the naval guardroom. The naval guardroom received a message, and they dispatched a land rover, which arrived as the audible sounded. The sailors checked the outside of the building and found it apparently secure. Then, they made a call to the building's key holder, a man named Burns, and he agreed to come. After satisfying themselves, the building was secure; the sailors left to continue their patrol inside the building and out of sight. The auto security cameras switched on and began recording.

Five minutes had passed before the key holder's car pulled up at the main gate, now locked and guarded by two Ministry of Defence Police officers armed with semi-automatic weapons.

He identified himself as Gary Burns. The guard checked the name on his roster and opened the gate. Five additional minutes later, two shore patrol officers accompanied Burns as he unlocked the museum and entered. Earlier, Caroline had experienced a feeling of dread in the replica section of the hull, which was one of the three rooms in the museum containing the artifacts. Burns turned on the lights and crossed to a small office to check the camera monitors. He found it surprising that the lights were on and the camera monitors were recording. The counter read 26 minutes. As he prepared to rewind the tape, a sharp cry rang out from the main hall.

"Oi you, stop right there."

Burns turned around and heard another voice.

"What's up Barry? What did you see?"

By the time Burns reached the display hall, he found the two naval ratings nervously holding drawn pistols.

"Somebody's here, sir. I saw a figure run into the hall."

The sailor immediately unclipped his personal radio

"Yellow Two, intruders on site at the Mary Rose Museum. Need backup."

Someone made a call to the Portsmouth Police centre. The immediate response prompted a quick redirection to the inside patrols. The police surrounded the building in 4 minutes. Burns had retreated outside the main door and was quickly approached by the duty inspector. He listened as the sailor related what he had seen. The inspector made several calls for the intruder, *'yo come out'*. There was no response. At which time, the handler released a police dog from its lead and encouraged it to bound into the building.

"Go get him Rex."

The dog needed no further encouragement and bounded through the door and into the building, barking loudly. Outside, the crew waited for the screams and shouts that would signify contact, but there was nothing. Even the dog stopped barking. After about two minutes had elapsed, the inspector dog handler and three sailors entered. A pitiful whimpering led them to the dog, now curled up and shaking. The hall seemed suddenly cold.

Despite the dog's reluctance, the dog handler reattached the lead and led the dog out of the building, requiring virtually dragging it. With no sign of an intruder, Burns returned to the office to replay the tape. Now he had an attentive audience.

At first, the tape showed nothing amiss, then movement from the bottom left-hand corner of the screen, a figure, slightly diffused, as are most images of these types. The figure moved slowly and did not look round to face the camera, denying the watchers a chance of seeing its face. It disappeared from view, but another figure quickly replaced it, and then a third. The security team watched, spellbound, as more and more figures were moving around the hall. This was, of course, impossible. The building was secure. No sign of any break in and there was clearly no one present now. Yet there they were.

Burns tried stopping and starting the video but it did not clear the images, then they dissipated. Light flooded the monitor screen, and seconds later images of Burns appeared, crossing the hall and heading for the office. He disappeared while the two accompanying sailors moved apart. For a few moments, all seemed normal. Then the screen picked up a clearer image, a man in a white shirt and a leather type waistcoat. It darted out of sight as the sailor turned and raised his pistol. There was no audio on the cameras, so they could only surmise this was the moment that the sailor challenged the figure. The camera recorded the party leaving and the pause. Burns attempted to shut it off, but the MOD police inspector intervened.

"No, leave it running; let's see what happened when the dog enters. Burns advanced the tape at double speed to that point. The dog entered swiftly and was obviously barking, and then it stopped and turned around rapidly, backing away, and curled up shaking."

Burns stopped the tape. No one said anything for a short while. The enormity of what the tape revealed sank in.

....

"Dad, it's Debbie, just a quickie; have you heard from Caroline De Winter recently?"

Geoffrey smiled to himself, but did not answer the question directly, instead firing one off of his own.

"That's an odd question. Why are you asking?"

"Well, we got a phone call from Professor Walker yesterday, shortly after you left. He is trying to reach her, and we think she might be in Portsmouth.

The reply surprised her father, who now thought he had apparently misjudged her.

"Interesting. Did he say why he was looking for her?"

Debbie realised he was being evasive, but played along.

"Not really. He said he had uncovered something further in a case he was interested in, and asked if we heard from her, to ask her to call him."

Geoffrey agreed, but said little else. Debbie thanked him and hung up. David, of course, had been listening on the speakerphone. Debbie smiled to herself.

"Oh, I guess we now know where dad was last night."

David kissed her on the cheek.

"You reckon?"

"Oh, I know Dad; if he hadn't seen her, he would have said so, right out. I would give a month's pay to know what this new information is all about."

Geoffrey's intrigue was clear. Like his daughter, he was never one to let an opportunity slide. As soon as he hung up on Debbie, he picked the phone up again and dialled the number Caroline had supplied. A female voice answered.

"The Royal Maritime Club; how can I help?"

"Thank you. Can you put me through to Mrs Caroline De Winter, room 17?"

....

Four hours had passed since Debbie's call when she heard a car pull up outside. She glanced out of the window and instantly recognised Caroline's Gold Mercedes. She called out to David with a smugness that she totally could not suppress.

"Dads here and he's with Caroline."

She greeted them at the door.

"Dad, and Caroline, well, this is a pleasant surprise."

Geoffrey looked past her and toward David before replying,

"Isn't it just?"

David shook his head, smiled, and said nothing.

Caroline was carrying a small folder that contained a sheet of paper, a computer printout of an email. As Yet, she had not read it fully, but now she did so, while Geoffrey filled in the story.

"Caroline is staying in Portsmouth for a few days at a hotel near Gun Wharf Quays. She called Sir Michael, and he sent her this email regarding the ring. He's been doing research. Caroline brought it over this morning, and I printed it off for her."

Caroline finished the email and handed it to Geoffrey.

A person designated the email as confidential.

To Mrs Caroline De Winter it read;

During further research into the origins of the ring David recently bought, I have uncovered a letter that may have some new insight into its origins. The document, buried deep in the Tudor Archives, was a letter written to Henry from the pope and it mentioned a gift, a ring that came from the Vatican treasury. (The full inventory remains secret to this day.) The letter didn't provide much detail about the ring, except that it was a stunning gold and emerald creation made by French artisans. It was commissioned to honor Joan of Arc for her leadership in the French victory against the English in 1429, with the claim that she was divinely guided. After her execution, those who opposed the Roman Catholic Church considered the ring a powerful symbol. And they locked it away for safekeeping until they sent it as a peace offering to King Henry VIII.'

'Had the pope expected the king would agree to drop his efforts to annual his marriage to Catherine, it appeared to have had the opposite effect. Henry presented the ring to Anne as his wedding gift and married her. After, the head of the Church of England, the Archbishop Cramer, declared the marriage to Catherine to be invalid, without waiting for a final decision from the pope.'

'This revelation was unexpected. Previously, it was assumed that Henry had crafted the ring as a wedding gift for Anne when they got married. The revelation that it came from the Vatican, opened up more questions.'

David was frustrated because if this had been a criminal case today, he would have simply asked the pope about why they presented the ring and its significance. Since he couldn't simply inquire with the pope today, he had to rely on centuries-old letters and manuscripts. Thank God for Google.

'At the time of Queen Anne's coronation, the Pope was Clemente VII, who at this time was virtually a prisoner of Charles V, the French Monarch who was also the nephew of Henrys first wife, Catharine of Aragon. Unsurprisingly, the King would not look favourably on the idea of his aunt being booted from the English Royal family, so began a long drawn out investigation of Henrys request. Committees and emissaries carried out the investigation, while Henry grew more impatient. It was during this time that one emissary had visited Henry with the gift; coincidently it was shortly after the visit that Anne's fidelity and allegiance to Henry came into question. The instigator was the Kings High Chancellor, Thomas Cromwell.'

'To his analytical police mind, a picture was emerging. The Catholic Church would have good reason to resent Henry's snub of the pope's gift and its subsequent use in what they considered being an unholy marriage. They may want to reclaim it. The Protestants, would see it as a great rallying cry, if they were to rise against the king. And in Henry's court, the Protestants would also mean the King's Chancellor, Thomas Cromwell. Obviously, Cromwell would have tried desperately to recover the ring, but fell out of favour with Henry, and subsequently also lost his head on the same scaffold. He went to his death knowing the ring was still out there.'

Caroline waited until Geoffrey had finished reading before speaking.

"All this time I have wondered whether the dark force stalking me was actually the King, but that would not make sense. Thomas Cromwell is a stronger candidate. Geoff, in your profession; you would say he would have both opportunity and motive."

....

The Mary Rose Museum remained closed the following morning. A notice on the door apologised for the inconvenience, quoting maintenance issues, and stated the museum would reopen the following day. Inside, a team of both police and Trust members were checking the exhibit hall and taking samples. They did not issue any statements. Instead, they informally told other dockworkers that there had been a severe chemical spill during the conservation work on some exhibits, which required thorough cleaning before allowing the public back in.

Police had taken the original security camera film, and it was being meticulously examined by their media experts, frame by frame. There appeared to be nothing wrong with the film or cameras, which were tested. The sudden drop in temperature reported by the key holder and naval team remained unexplained. The exhibits were in a temperature controlled environment, and this was working perfectly. Of course, it occurred to many that what the video showed was not a physical presence, but a supernatural one. The videographer, DC Steve Sweet, captured some images from the screen, and then put them through enhancing software. The result was startling; it showed a male figure dressed in what appeared to be Elizabethan clothing. There was no clear shot of the face; however, he appeared to be sporting a beard. He printed off the images and placed all but two in a Manilla envelope. These, he felt, were worthy of further study outside the confines of the MOD Police.

Chapter 18

Dark Days for the Spencer's

Despite working almost full time on the research project tracing the ring, both Debbie and David were now looking forward to getting back to work. Debbie had called the station, and was told she was being crewed with another female officer, to a Southsea patrol area encompassing Clarence Pier and the dockyard entrance. David would not know his assignment until he reported in. As often happens, they were working different shift patterns; David 8 to 4, and Debbie 2 to 10. When David left for Portswood, Debbie took the time to review some data collected. Her mind worked methodically, like most police officers, and she had prepared spreadsheets on dates and times. At 10:15 AM the post arrived, and as she sorted through the mail, one letter caught her eye, it had American stamps on it, and as is normal for US letters, it had the sender's name and address on it. It was from New York, from a Mrs Strauss. Immediately, Debbie knew this was the data David had been waiting on. He had, in fact, been expecting an email. She knew she should wait until this evening to open it, but was sure David would not object. The letter was a personal one from a member of the Strauss family.

'Dear Mr Spencer,

Thank you for your letter regarding the history of the ring that once belonged to my Great, Great Grandmother; I was most intrigued to read of the connection with the famous Confederate General, James Longstreet. I have searched the family records and found that my great, Great Grandfather Isadora did, in fact, know the General, and found a copy receipt dated May 6, 1867, for a gold dress ring set with 7 emeralds.

From this description, I am pretty comfortable that this is the ring you are researching. Also, I have enclosed a copy of the receipt General Longstreet got for the ring at the Great Exhibition in London. I trust this may be of service in your continued research.

Regards,

A.G. Strauss'

Debbie looked at the receipt. John Simpson and Son, Bespoke Jewellers, at 20 The Strand, London, headed the receipt.

Debbie immediately entered the details into her computer. But the address now showed a meeting room. This would take deeper research. She left the paperwork on the computer desk and then called her father; there was no reply, so she left a message on the answerphone. She then called David, but similarly got an engaged tone. This was frustrating.

Meanwhile, Geoffrey had met Caroline for coffee at his favourite café in Gun Wharf Quays. He had hoped for a quiet morning, but unfortunately, Dr Ruth Walters was also in the café and spotted him shortly after he arrived. She approached, and wished him a pleasant day, but seemed more interested in his companion. With an air of almost resignation, Geoffrey stood up and introduced both Caroline and Dr Walters. Both registered surprise. It was Ruth who spoke first.

"Mrs De Winter, I am delighted to meet you. My colleague Sir Michael Walker has often spoken of you. I understand you are a paranormal investigator. Is that correct?"

Caroline smiled weakly and countered.

"I would accept that, and I Know Sir Michael has often spoken of you. Dr Walters, I understand you trained under him. And I know Geoffrey's daughter has often mentioned you. Her husband is a patient of yours, I understand."

Ruth looked a little surprised and replied.

"Well, I'm afraid I cannot discuss any patient's that I may or may not have, for confidentiality reasons."

Geoffrey quickly interceded.

"Quite so, Dr Walters, and I'm sure neither of us would ever suggest anything to the contrary."

If Geoffrey had hoped that would end the conversation, he was to be disappointed; Caroline had no intention of letting this opportunity slip.

"Well, Dr Walters, would you care to join us, anyway? I am sure we can get along perfectly, referencing nothing that would breach either of our desires to keep confidences."

Ruth accepted, and the conversation turned to general conceptions of psychiatry and psychology, much to Geoffrey's dismay.

Meanwhile, at Portswood Station, David was studying the latest intelligence files from the anti-terrorist squad. Most were just a general alert on heightened tensions following the 9/11 attacks a month earlier; nothing specific, but there was one line that caught his eye.

Security level at military bases has risen to amber status. They mentioned the Naval base at Portsmouth as a potential target. Still, it was no genuine concern. In the event of an incident, the dockyard had armed security, and they could effectively handle it. Meanwhile, Debbie had resumed her work on her research, particularly regarding Emily Spencer. After the death of her husband, there was no mention of her in England, but an entry was found in a French account of Charles' 1' 1st son, who was in exile in France. The list of those names of his court in exile listed a lady-in-waiting, Mrs Emily Spencer. The date of the entry was July 1652. A few more links on Google and Wikipedia threw up entries showing the same name, as present at his coronation in 1660, but then nothing, until a report of her death in 1671. Again, there was no mention of the ring. She entered the details on the database and switched it off.

At 1:30, Debbie left the house in uniform and drove to Portsmouth Central Police station in Winston Churchill Avenue.

The shift began as usual, with the Duty Sergeant announcing incidents that were being handed over from the morning shift. The Duty Sergeant allocated Debbie Panda 1, and she crewed with the popular probationer Jenny Wilson, a 19-year-old in her second year of service. Debbie had crewed with her before, and the two got on pretty well. Some probationers were unpopular, because they did not know too much outside training school, but Jenny was different.

Debbie was not her regular tutor constable, but had done 4 patrols with her. Before commencing the patrol, Debbie put on her protective vest and helped Jenny secure hers. These vests were available for all patrol officers, but only during heightened threats were they usually worn.

Debbie disliked hers because its bulk restricted movement. A complaint many female officers had. Jenny had noticed that Debbie's vest differed slightly from hers, it was about the same size but the shape was more fitted, it also looked considerably older. Sensing her question, Debbie smiled.

"No, it's not regulation. It's one batch the US police sent over in 1994. David ordered two, and, after we got married in 98, he gave me one. Said it offered more protection than the British ones. Haven't worn it too much, but since the twin towers attack, I keep it in my car. Today I wore it, as we had the order to wear them, and most of all, it will keep David off my back. I'd just as soon as you didn't broadcast it."

Jenny replied

"Don't worry; your secret is safe with me."

As usual, the patrol was pretty routine. The prime tourist season was winding down, and the seafront between South Parade and Clarence piers was fairly clear of traffic. The large funfair at Clarence pier shut down for the winter, and Debbie eagerly anticipated going home to David to see if he had made any progress.

The area was getting dark at 7 PM. It was half an hour after sunset when the radio cracked to life.

"Panda 1, report of suspicious vehicle outside main dock gates at HMS warrior on the hard; described as a dark coloured Volvo estate containing 4 males. Informant, MOD Police."

Debbie responded,

"Panda 1 received, on route, ETA five minutes."

It took them actually less than four, but as they reached the docks, Debbie saw the Volvo. Debbie saw the Volvo parked on the hard, close to the berthed warship. The driver started the engine when he saw her signal to turn into the car park area. Without lights, the car sped up forward, causing Debbie to swerve violently to avoid a collision. It swung onto the road with a squeal of tyres. Debbie threw the Ford Escort into a donut style spin, sending loose gravel across the hard, and set off in pursuit.

She threw the beacon light switch on, and Jenny grabbed the radio.

"Panda 1, in pursuit of suspect, Volvo estate, licence number Romeo, six, three, six, delta, mike, Romeo, four males, IC4 west on park Road."

The Volvo was picking up speed, and Debbie guessed it was heading for the M25 motorway, as it swung left into Anglesey road. Then the car made a serious error. It sped across the junction of Queen Street without stopping and collided with a single-decker city bus. The impact spun the Volvo around and deposited it on the grass verge, close to the cathedral. Jenny called out the location on the radio.

"Suspect vehicle crashed outside the cathedral."

It was the last call the young 19-year-old would ever make.

As she and Debbie exited the patrol car, a passenger window on the Volvo opened and the muzzle of an Armalite style automatic weapon appeared. Spitting flames, a hail of bullets slammed into Jenny, knocking her back into the seat. More rounds struck Debbie, three of them in the chest and one grazing her head. The force of the bullets' impact threw her sideways, depositing her body about 7 yards from the shattered police car.

The Volvo drove back onto the road and sped away, its front end badly crumpled. As it sped up from the scene, other motorists rushed to the fallen police women. Debbie was gasping, hardly able to breathe now. Her head was throbbing, and her vision clouded. Coughing, she rolled over on her front and saw Jenny lying dazed in the front seat of the Escort. She reached out and tried to tell her to get clear. But her lack of breath reduced her words to a whisper.

"Get out Jenny, now, get out."

There was no response, as smoke billowed from the engine before the car disappeared in a blinding flash of flame as the fuel tank exploded. For Debbie, everything now went black.

....

David had settled down for the evening to watch a game show on TV, and had just got up to get a coffee during the commercial break. While he was making his way back to the sofa, the screen changed, and a breaking news title appeared. A Sky news announcer came on.

"We are receiving reports of an incident in Portsmouth showing that a terror-related incident has seriously injured two police officers. We have a team on the way, and will update you as soon as possible. Now, back to our regular program."

David turned off the TV and moved for the phone, which suddenly rang before he reached it.

Anxiously, he picked up the receiver.

"David, it's Chris Harper. You better get to the General. Debbie's been shot, and she's in a bad way."

It took David less than 7 minutes to reach the hospital. A news TV van was outside with a reporter, repeatedly trying to ask questions, and being all but ignored. David flashed his warrant card and entered the main entrance. On arrival at reception, Supt. Hawke was already there, along with two other senior officers, and Geoffrey, also Caroline, which no doubt Debbie would not have found at all surprising. Hawke approached him.

"She's in the ICU at the moment, David, and they are working on her. We are waiting for the surgeon now. Reports are sketchy; she and WPC Wilson were in pursuit of a suspect vehicle and came under fire from an automatic rifle, an AK 47, judging by the spent cases at the scene. Their panda crashed and exploded, throwing Debbie clear before the explosion. Jenny Wilson, who was also hit several times by the gunfire, died in the explosion.

David said nothing for a moment, then stammered.

"Any word on the suspects?"

Hawke shook his head.

"Jenny gave us the car number and described the occupants as 4 IC4s. We think it was heading for the M25."

David nodded, he looked totally shattered, Geoffrey approached them nodding to Hawke, who discreetly stepped back.

"Alright David, there's nothing you, or I, can do now, but to allow the Doctors to do their job. It's a tough waiting game, but I know what it's like. I spent some time in this very hospital with Debbie's mother 4 years ago. You may remember."

David did and said somewhat hoarsely.

"Yes, I do, and she didn't make it, did she?"

A uniformed police officer approached Hawke and saluted.

"Excuse me sir, the press are getting impatient, and are asking when they can expect a statement."

Hawke glared at the officer.

"As far as I am concerned, you can tell them to fuck off."

Then he quickly added.

"No, constable, you had better not. Have Jenny's next of kin been informed?"

The Officer replied

"Yes sir, the duty Inspector Mrs Roberts is with them. I believe they are on their way to the mortuary."

"Alright tell the press we will have an update for them at 8 PM."

The officer saluted and left. Hawke then approached Geoffrey.

"Damn vultures. I have little time for them, Geoff."

Geoffrey smiled

"One of the more unsavoury aspects of this job, but we are stuck with them."

David looked at Caroline and noted she had been quiet since he had arrived.

He spoke to her,

"Tell me honestly Caroline, is this the result of that damn ring? She's kept it under lock and key and has never worn it. Did I start this whole incident when I bought her the ring?"

Caroline looked up at him with tears in her eyes.

"Honestly, I do not know. It's possible, I suppose, but equally, it could just be a tragic co-incidence. A police officer's job is not exactly the safest of professions. I am sure you knew that, both of you. As for Debbie, she is in the best hands she could be in, God's hands. Does it surprise you to hear that even mediums acknowledge a higher power?"

The conversation came to a halt as a gowned surgeon entered the reception, removing his surgical mask.

"David Spencer?"

David quickly got to his feet.

"Well, young man, your wife is one tough cookie. She has a bullet wound to the head. It's superficial, but it is causing pressure on the brain. That is keeping her in a coma at present. She also has three wounds to

her chest area where her vest took the brunt of the bullets. We have a penetration of around one inch, far less than I would expect. She also has 1st degree burns on her face assumedly from the blast. We have bagged up her personal effects, uniform and such. I'm sure investigators will need them as evidence.

"What's her chances Doctor?"

Emotion was clear in David's question.

"Well, she's stable at the moment, and will remain in a medically induced coma. We will obviously continue to monitor her, but we expect she will most likely recover fully in a few weeks. She is a very lucky woman."

It took David a few moments for the Doctor's assessment to sink in, before he replied

"Thank you Doctor; how long before I can see her?"

"Well, she is in a coma at the moment, medically induced. The impact of the bullets has caused severe bruising and there is some swelling around the heart area. I would expect she will be conscious again by tomorrow afternoon. If she continues to make progress, we will move her from the ICU in a couple of days. You know officer; I have seen wounds from an AK47 weapon before, while serving in the territorials in the Gulf War. Her ballistic vest did some job; she clearly owes her life to it."

David knew Hawke was listening, but at that moment did not care.

"I realise that Doctor, if she had been wearing the regulation stab proof vest, she would be dead. The one she had on is an American law enforcement level 3, supplied privately from US Law enforcement agencies in the mid-90s. It is secondhand, and designed to stop handguns, not high calibre bullets like the 7.62 AK round."

Geoffrey came over.

"We cannot do any more here at present. You best go on home. I'll take your car back, and you can ride with Caroline."

Hawke now came over.

"Your father-in-law is right, David. Get home and get a good night's sleep. I'll call your DS. You are on compassionate leave until further notice, and don't make me have to make that an order."

David followed Caroline and Geoffrey out of the entrance. Hawke had begun his press briefing, so no one tried to interview them.

"Nice car Caroline."

David remarked as they left the car park. It was a clumsy attempt to talk about something other than Debbie, and Caroline immediately saw through it.

"Yes, it is, but I don't think you feel like talking about cars tonight, do you?"

David looked slightly annoyed

"What do you suggest, a story of a ring that kills people?"

Caroline took no offence and replied softly and with a tone of concern.

"No, but Debbie has survived. The other poor girl had no connection with her, or the ring. She died because of a terrorist act. That same act could have taken Debbie, but didn't I would like to see if there was a reason. I know you think it was the vest, and that would be logical, but I am not so sure. I'm only alive today because a good friend left a cell phone in my flat, and came back to retrieve it just as a fire was starting in the flat below. I don't have all the answers, but I would like to dig deeper. And for the record, I think that your research into the ring is a good thing. It may yet provide a link that, as you coppers say, cracks the case."

David nodded.

"As a matter of fact, I got some more information in today's post from the Strauss family in New York that appears to link the ring to a confederate general who bought it at the great Victorian exhibition in London. I also got the details of the seller. I was going to do some digging on that, when..."

He hesitated before continuing.

"When Debbie got off shift."

Geoffrey was now in front of them, and leading the way. Ten minutes later, they pulled onto David's Drive. Once inside, David hurried to the kitchen, announcing he would make the coffee. The red light was flashing on the answerphone, but he ignored it. David handed the papers on the ring, which he had got that morning, over to Caroline and Geoffrey, who both read them carefully. David also showed them the spreadsheet that he and Debbie had been working on. There was no doubt the pattern was emerging. Out of everyone, Caroline was the only one who seemed to make sense of it, but her explanation was too unbelievable to really be considered. Geoffrey was prepared to have a go. Once they were sitting down, he spoke. He addressed Caroline with his comments.

"You seem to have found a common thread with this. Now if the ring is the source of this string of tragedies, surely the person, or persons, who cursed the ring, is long dead and buried. Why would it still keep such power?"

"Well, before, I do not think it is the ring. It is someone guiding events; an Entity, or spirit, if you like. My hunch is that he seeks the ring's destruction, needs it to no longer exist. And his attempts to destroy it have led to these deaths."

David was still 't convinced.

"So are you saying that these victims were all just collateral damage, including my former self, John Grainger, in fact, the entire crew of the Mary Rose? That's pretty hard to swallow, Caroline."

"Yes it is, until you remember that spirits cannot physically move objects, they cannot destroy the ring by, say, throwing it in a furnace."

David had a question and wasted no time in asking it.

"What about Poltergeists? They move things around, don't they? Isn't that why they call them mischievous spirits?"

Caroline was unphased.

"That's what they call them, but they are wrong. Poltergeists are not mischievous at all, more like attention seekers, making their presence

known, and they do not physically move objects, they displace the surrounding air, causing movements. Like creating a sudden vacuum in front of, or behind, something, causing air and the object to rush in and fill the gap. This case is unusual, because it involves such a long gap, almost 500 years."

With Debbie no longer available to seek advice from, David now turned to his Father in Law.

"So what do we do now Geoff, there must be a way of stopping this madness?"

He looked at Caroline.

"It's a fair question; Caroline, what do you suggest?"

The same question had been troubling her for a month now; she got up from her chair.

"We cannot let this situation go on. I think I may be able to stop it. I need to confront the Spirit direct and find out what is behind this."

Now Geoffrey spoke up, with his voice raised in almost anger.

"No Caroline, you cannot risk it again. It's too dangerous. Find another way."

David turned to her

"What does he mean, dangerous? In what way?"

Geoffrey answered for him.

"She tried that before and almost died. I cannot risk that happening to her."

Caroline smiled and kissed him lightly on the cheek.

"That's very chivalrous of you, sweetie, but this is the only way. I will need some help, though. I have to make a call."

....

After Caroline and Geoffrey left, David ran the messages back on the answerphone. As he expected, many were expressing support and prayers for Debbie's recovery. One, however, was not.

He played the message back several times.

'*Hello DC Spencer, sorry to intrude at this time, but I need to see you, or at the very least, talk to you. My name is DC Swift, MOD Police, photographic section. We had a possible break in at the Mary Rose Museum a couple of nights back. Now I understand that you and your wife have recently been conducting research together with a mutual acquaintance, Mrs Caroline De Winter. If this is correct, please return this call and I can explain further.*'

David noted the number. At first he had called the number later, but knowing that Debbie may regain consciousness as early as tomorrow, and that Caroline was about to undertake a dangerous contact, he decided not to wait.

He dialled the number.

There was a brief pause.

"*Hi, Steve Sweet.*"

David took a deep breath before replying,

"*Hello, Steve, DC Spencer Portswood CID, I got your message. Sorry for the delay in replying, it's been hectic round here; so what have you got?*"

"*Well, first, how is your wife? Our force is cut up, as we originated the call. We're pretty cut up at that young WPCs death?*"

David knew the officer was genuine and quickly replied.

"*Well, thank you for that, and I assure you no one, least of all my wife, or WPC Wilson Family, in any way holds you responsible. So what was this break in about?*"

"*Well, at first we thought it was a false alarm, no sign of damage or a break in. We waited for the Key holder, as per protocol, and accompanied him along with a few ratings. Inside, one rating confronted an individual in the main display hall who was armed, but did not discharge their weapon. We secured the area until additional support and a K9 unit arrived.*

Something scared the dog out of its wits. Later, we ran back the security tapes. They show something totally beyond explanation. The tapes

are not available as we store them under a security classification. However,
I got some screen shots. Which they don't know about yet. I am hoping to
keep it that way. I am sure you can appreciate why."

David did, only too well, and also knew he had to get a hold of the
pictures before anyone started asking awkward questions.

He gave his address and asked him to call round as soon as
practicable; the reply surprised him.
"Well, I know it's late, but truthfully, I want to get rid of these at the
earliest opportunity. I can be round there in 20 minutes."

David agreed. Normally he would have run a check on this officer
to check he was who he claimed to be, but doing so may raise suspicions
with the MOD Police command. Under the circumstances, he would
just have to see it through.

Twenty-two minutes elapsed before David saw the Capri pull up
outside. The driver was a young man in his mid-twenties. He did not
appear to be carrying anything and was the car's only occupant. David
opened the door as he approached.
"Come in Steve."
The MOD officer needed no second invitation. He looked a little
nervous. Once inside, he extended his hand, which David took.
"Thank you David. It was good of you to see me so late."
He produced an envelope and handed it over.
David motioned him to sit down and opened the envelope,
switching on the reading lamp as he did so. He carefully scanned each
one before putting them back.
"And the security camera took these in a locked and secure building?"
Sweet nodded and added.
"There is no reporting of hauntings or other supernatural events
taking place before. But; and I am jumping to conclusions here, one of
my colleagues saw a woman he recognised a couple of weeks ago at the

Museum. Caroline De Winter, who is apparently well known in the paranormal investigator circuit, was the one who reported no hauntings or other supernatural events taking place before. He is interested in such stuff. She was suddenly ill, and her companion took care of her. Another colleague also identified ex Chief Inspector Hawthorne, a relative of yours, or so I believe."

David nodded, now beginning to catch on.

"My Father-in-law. Ok, Steve, pretty good work. Your hunch is correct. But you do not know the entire story."

David narrated the facts as he knew them and showed him Debbie's spreadsheets for the next hour. He ended the meeting with a statement of support.

"Thank you for showing me these. I really understand the risk you took with your job. I'll pass them on to Caroline, but will not mention your name. I think these pictures may well explain the whole affair."

Chapter 19

Confrontation

David entered the ICU with some trepidation. Debbie was lying still on her bed; she looked like a broken doll. Heavy bandages covered the top of her head, and a cotton wool pad was taped to her right cheek. The medical staff attached a saline drip to her left arm. She turned her head towards him and half smiled, wincing at the obvious pain she was enduring.

He sat beside her and gently touched her hand.

"Hi sweetie, fancy meeting a girl like you in a dump like this."

Debbie gave a half smile and whispered hoarsely.

"If I had known you were coming, I'd have tidied up a bit."

David smiled and gently squeezed her hand. Before replying,

"It's great to see you, sweetheart. I'm not supposed to stay long, but to hell with that. The entire force is rooting for you. Is there anything you need, or anyone I need to contact?"

Debbie's expression changed as she looked at her husband.

"I've been asking, but no one is saying anything. Jenny's dead, isn't she?"

David nodded

"She never stood a chance Deb, she was likely dead before the Panda blew up. I'm so sorry."

Debbie nodded in resignation.

"I knew it; those guys had an AK assault rifle, and her stab vest offered no protection."

"The surgeon told me that your vest saved your life. It took most of the impact, with minor penetration. I thank god that you had it on, and that I ordered it for you when they became available."

There was an awkward silence, and David changed the subject.

"By the way, it seems you were right about your dad, and Caroline. They appear to be way more than just friends."

Debbie smiled weakly.

"I'm glad. Dad needs someone back in his life. He's been lonely for far too long. It's not good to be alone in these times; I think we will all be facing some big changes in the coming years. Bush's war on terror will probably affect us too, as well as America. Speaking of Caroline, I would really like to see her. Will she be coming in later?"

....

At the same time as David was comforting his badly injured wife, Caroline was back at Geoffrey's house, and they were not alone. Phillip Watson had travelled down from Surrey, and preparations were underway for Caroline to make contact. Importantly, David had given her the photo screen shots from Steve Sweet. She stared at them for a few minutes.

"These are pretty convincing, Geoffrey. I know now that my first suspicions were right. This figure is recognisable from many portraits I have seen. To stop him, I must make a deal with him, an offer he can hardly refuse."

Phillip gave her a quick embrace.

"Watch yourself Caroline. This spirit is not the usual kind we encounter. He is dangerous, and evil. I will watch over you, and will break the séance if I have to. But not until I have to; I realise how important this is to you."

He checked the recorder and camera, and more importantly, the ECG sensors attached to Caroline's torso. They would record her vital signs, and give warning of overstress. Finally, he turned to Geoffrey.

"Now, just to recap; if Caroline makes contact, she cannot converse with either of us. No matter what you see and think, it is vital that you say, or do, nothing to interfere. To do so would seriously endanger Caroline, and she does not need any other problems right now."

Caroline chipped in.

"Now listen to him, Geoff. I know you find all this pretty bizarre, but we know what we are doing. Trust me on this. I would have preferred that you were not here, but barring you would have caused me even more headaches."

She smiled, and her tone softened.

"It's OK to wish me luck."

Geoffrey kissed her on the forehead, and then on impulse on the lips. She smiled as he whispered;

"Good luck darling, I'll be right here."

He resumed his seat and Phillip darkened the room.

Caroline closed her eyes. For a moment, there was silence, then she spoke.

"Sir Thomas Cromwell, we need to talk. This has gone on too long."

Phillip stared at his instruments and watched for any signs of temperature or pressure variations.

The radiation meter clicked momentarily. Caroline spoke again.

"Do not ignore me, Thomas; you have been chasing this ring for centuries now. You have brought great pain and sorrow to many who did not know you and had no way of understanding. I do. I am the only one who can help, as I do not care about your damn trinket. You cannot hide from me, and I do not fear you."

A sudden chill swept through the room. As the instruments burst to life, they slammed Caroline back in her chair and a cloud of vapor began to form above her. Then she spoke, or at least her lips moved, but the voice was not hers, a deep masculine voice, menacing and direct.

"You dare to address me, wench. You know who I am."

In her own voice, Caroline delivered her reply.

"I know who you were; you betrayed your king, and the Lady Anne. Your pathetic attempts to conceal the ring from your king cost you your life. Now you are nothing, an empty, lost soul who desperately seeks to right a wrong that cannot be fixed. I alone can solve your problem and destroy the ring forever. But I will only do it in return for a pledge from you, yes, you, Thomas Cromwell, Lord Chancellor, of the realm who has fallen so far. You have no choice. Every death you bring about condemns your soul deeper into the fires of hell. For you, there can be no peace, just the eternal fires of damnation. So, do you have the courage to accept my offer? I will not make the offer again.

The cloud above Caroline was now condensing, and a face was appearing. The same face recorded on the Security cameras at the Museum. It wore an expression of controlled anger. Phillip checked the sensors read out from the contacts on Caroline's body. They recorded a rise in heart rate and respiration.

"Why would you destroy the ring? It can grant you riches beyond your imagination. So it has been since its creation. None have had the courage to destroy it. Why would you be any different from your ancestors?"

Caroline's reply was direct.

"I am the conduit between the dead and the living, between your world and mine. I give comfort and assurance to those who pass over. You are a threat to the peace of all of us. What value is this ring compared to that. Once I destroy the ring, your quest is over; you can also make your peace with God. The choice is yours. Now is the time to make it."

There was no reply. Phil watched as the temperature and pressure readings dropped. After a minute, he looked up.

"Readings back to zero. He's gone."

All eyes were now on Caroline, who remained motionless. Her vital signs remained slightly down, but not alarmingly so. She opened her eyes and scanned the room before fixing her gaze on Geoffrey, who was the first to speak.

"Are you alright girl?"

Caroline managed a weak smile.

"I've had better days, honey. That's a fact."

Phil handed her a glass of water, which she took immediately, gulping down half of it in one go.

After a moment, she answered the question they were all waiting to hear.

"I think I got through to him. He knows he now has a chance to end the torment, not just for us, but for him as well. There are many tormented souls with him, including the crew of the Mary Rose and countless others. The ring here is the key. For 500 years, it has been an obsession. He blames everything he has lost on it; the trust of the King, the wrath of the Pope, his fall from grace, and his eventual death. He may just call off the war. He may still believe he can destroy it himself. We may not know for a while. Dreams from David and Margaret may provide a clue. It's a waiting game."

Geoffrey now gave voice to his thoughts.

"Well, I am pretty sure neither David nor my daughter ever want to see the ring again. I vote we just throw it into an industrial furnace, or take a blowtorch to it, to hell with the value."

Caroline shook her head.

"That would be a big mistake, Geoff. You, of all people, should know you cannot give into blackmail. I have an idea. But I will need to discuss it with both you and Debbie when she is well enough to be released. Cromwell's spirit will not be far away. My advice, for what it's worth, is that we do nothing until then. Leave the ring where it is and await developments."

....

To David, at least it came as no surprise when Caroline checked out of her hotel and moved in with Geoffrey. With Debbie now out of ICU and back in the main ward, visiting hours were more relaxed.

The dreams had stopped, and he was at last able to resume his attempts to complete the history of the ring. Geoffrey and Caroline had pitched in too, concentrating their search on the years of Charles the Second, and the date of Emily Spencer's death in 1671.

David started from the other direction, concentrating on the great Victorian exhibition, and the Jeweller who had sold the ring to Longstreet, John Simpson and Son of the Strand, London.

He had already established the premises were no longer there. So his next step was a search of the company records. The company records listed the business as being in operation from 1825 to 1866. Further research showed, the Company enjoyed Royal Patronage, and carried a Royal Appointment crest. This showed they had, on at least one occasion, supplied Queen Victoria or her court with high quality Jewellery. That would at least explain why they were exhibiting at the Great Exhibition.

Then a clue appeared, a report of the company obtaining a quantity of Jewellery from the Estate of Admiral Robert James Spencer after his death in September 1839, but David could find no link. Doing the research suddenly turned a light on in his mind. The Battle of the Nile had featured in another family history. One he and Debbie had been researching long before the bad dreams, his own.

Quickly, he opened the desktop file marked ancestry. It took him directly to Ancestry.com, a five-year-old genealogy site that he and Debbie had joined, to trace their family tree. One entry there suddenly took on a whole new meaning. Ensign John Spencer promoted the First Lieutenant following his heroism at the battle of the Nile in 1798. John Spencer was David's Great, Great Grandfather.

Things were now getting just a little scary. One of his ancestors' relative had sold a quantity of Jewellery to the Jeweller, who had supplied the ring to James Longstreet. Was this just a co-incidence, if so, it was a pretty big one. David then carried out a search online, more in hope than expectation, for a catalogue of the auction under that date. At first there was nothing, then a small entry with an eBay link.

Someone listed a copy of the catalogue for sale under historic documents. The Ad was over a year old, and must therefore have been sold by now. Nevertheless, he clicked on the seller and sent a message, asking if the catalogue was still for sale, and if not, did they have a contact for the buyer? He explained his intention to determine whether a certain gold and emerald ring was listed. Now all he could do was wait. For now there was one other thing he needed to do. He picked up his phone and called Caroline.

....

Debbie was now looking a lot better, propped up in bed and checking her Facebook profile. David calling her Tonto rattled her somewhat as the bandage around her head had reduced to little more than a headband. Her left cheek still showed signs of blistering but appeared to be healing fast. David spent an hour with her this morning. Since Caroline's Séance, he had experienced no more dreams. He had decided not to say anything about his possible historic connection with the ring until he heard from the eBay seller.

Meanwhile, Geoffrey and Caroline were also making progress. That afternoon they invited David over, primarily to find out if Debbie was up to receiving visitors. Since Debbie's hospitalisation, they had been concentrating on Emily Spencer's death in 1671. After David's arrival, Caroline confirmed they had traced a daughter named Sarah Spencer as a surviving relative. It appears she was born to long after Harding's death and had no connection with the earlier Spencer's. Caroline's best guess was that Sarah was illegitimate, and Emily gave her the name Spencer to avoid any scandal.

Consulting her notes, Caroline continued

"She seems to have been a resourceful woman in her own right. We found a marriage entry for her to another Spencer in 1714, Christopher

Spencer; I would love to know the story of how they met. Anyhow, they did, and we traced three children to them. Emily, (After her Grandma no doubt) born in 1716, Susan in 1717, and the youngest, a boy named Robert, in 1721. So far, Robert is the only one we have extra info on. It seems he grew up in the Portsmouth area and joined the Navy. His bio on Wikipedia says he joined the Royal Navy in 1739 and rose through the ranks to become an admiral. He died in 1838, at 99."

David's visible shaking indicated that the possibility of coincidence was now almost nonexistent. Without comment, he handed Geoffrey a copy of the almost complete family tree. He read it and passed it to Caroline.

For a couple of minutes, everyone remained silent. Then David spoke up.

"It's not concrete, and I still have to hear from the catalogue seller, if he replies, but incredible as it seems, this ring has been following my family for over 500 years, leaving a trail of misery in its wake."

Geoffrey turned to Caroline.

"Is that possible Caroline, I mean, is there any precedent for that?"

Caroline stared at the data sheets and replied in almost a whisper.

"No, at least none that I know of, but it would explain a lot, even why we are all wrapped up in this affair. One thing I have kept secret until now, but I think it is time to share. I hope it will not change the way you feel about me, Geoff, or you, David. You see, I also have a family tree, and my name is distinct enough to track. It seems one of my distant ancestors owned a shop in Calais in the 16th century, and bought a distinct ring from the wife of a notorious executioner, the same one who dispatched Queen Anne Boleyn. And I believe it is the same ring now sitting in your safe, David."

She looked up at him with tears in her eyes.

"As I once told your wife, sometimes having second sight is a curse I could well do without."

David nodded understandingly as his phone suddenly buzzed. A Flashing symbol showed he had received an email. He clicked on the Icon, a brief message from the eBay seller.

"Hi David, sorry, I sold the Catalogue, but took a photocopy of it from my records. It shows a Tudor ring with 7 emeralds set in gold. I will scan the page and send it to your email. Cheers, Doug."

For a full minute, nobody spoke. David realised that together, they had closed the case. What Debbie would make of it was, of course, anybody's guess. He turned to Geoffrey.

"So what now? Do I cancel my appointments with Ruth? Stop all the therapy, and what about the ring?"

Geoffrey knew all eyes were now upon him, including Caroline's. He then spoke, giving his opinion, with no window dressing or attempt to minimise the situation.

"Well, Caroline put herself at risk of confronting the spirit of Thomas Cromwell. His obsession is to see the ring destroyed. So far, he has failed, and has no reason to stop trying. He has proved over the last four centuries that he has no concerns over how many die as a result. Caroline offered him a way out. Destruction of the ring in return for him stopping his rampage of hate, she has made it plain she will need to see proof of his acceptance of those terms. These are things you have to decide, and before much longer."

Caroline nodded in agreement, and added.

"Geoff is right, we do not own the ring, and I feel that my duty was to convey the warning from Joan and John to those who they were trying to reach. That, I have done. Frankly, the way forward is something I cannot advise you on. You and Debbie need to decide."

EPILOUGE

The wind was moderate, force 3 to 4 at an estimate. The small fishing boat was making good headway against the occasional whitecaps. It had cleared the harbour wall at Sally Port, and now was visible from both the historic Round Tower and Southsea Castle. On board, most of the 7 passengers were checking their equipment. David spencer had made a special request to the boat's skipper. He had already consulted him on the location and bearing. The boat skipper was a little puzzled.

"John, I acknowledge that it's only a minor detour, but the chart clearly marks the area as restricted. No diving, or fishing, and no anchoring. Can I ask, what's the point?"

David smiled.

"I just want to get an idea of her position, where she was when she went down, and get a couple of shots. Just throttle back to about 3 knots, so I can keep the camera steady."

The passengers, all police officers from the angling club, looked up as they heard the engine slow. They knew enough of this area to realise they could not fish here. The nearest fishable wreck was on an old WW1 submarine hulk, about two miles distant. David quickly reassured them.

"Don't panic, we are not stopping here, but I've always been interested in seeing the spot where the Mary Rose sank, just getting a couple of shots."

Fifty yards ahead, two conical buoys appeared. As they grew closer, they saw the faded letters, Mary Rose, still just visible on the rusted surface. Of course, there was no wreck there now. But it was still possible to see parts of it littered on the sea floor. The Mary Rose Trust had secured sole rights to the ship and any artefacts remaining, which was why the area was out of bounds. But with the bulk of the ship now ashore, diving expeditions were far less frequent. David took out the camera from its case and made some adjustments, some anglers, now took an interest. This was not in the plan. David spoke up.

"It was here that the ship went down, killing most of her crew. The sea was awash with drowned bodies, and good king Henry VII was watching from just over there."

He pointed at the buff stoned edifice of Southsea Castle, a mile to the north. As he had hoped, all eyes followed his finger. As they did so, David moved over to the gunwale, his hand gripping a small conical shell that he quietly dropped over the side. It struck the surface of the water, barely making a splash, and drew no reaction from the surrounding anglers. He watched as it tumbled down out of sight and thought he saw a flash of gold and gemstone, but probably not. He had sealed the ring inside the shell with a small wedge of mud. Satisfied, he took one more shot of the buoys, lowered the camera and nodded to the skipper, who nodded back and then opened the throttle. The boat surged forward and turned southeast towards the Nab Tower. On the sea floor, the shell bounced along the sandy bottom, unseen by human eyes. It slowly settled, and the sand and soft mud quickly covered it. David glanced at the buoys falling behind in the boat's wake, and then up to the scurrying clouds. He had kept his promise. Now he and Debbie could rest easier. He hoped that Cromwell's spirit, too, could now find his own eternal rest.

Meanwhile, 20 miles to the North West in a small churchyard, just outside the village of Romsey, Caroline De Winters' Mercedes pulled into the car park. She and Geoffrey remained in the front seat while Ian and Margaret climbed out of the rear. Caroline watched as they entered the churchyard, moving off to the left and right of the pathway. The couple began checking the faded and well weathered gravestones. After around 10 minutes, Ian called out, and Margaret ran over to join him.

Before them was a weathered gravestone half covered with brown moss and white lichens. The inscription was barely visible. Ian carefully cleared away the moss and wiped a moistened tissue over the letters. As the stone darkened, the words came into sharper relief.

Joan Spencer, 1521–1567, RIP; a simple, all but forgotten marker, in a dark and overgrown part of an ancient Hampshire churchyard. The Parish rector watched curiously from the church entrance, as Margaret knelt down and placed a spray of Hampshire roses on the ground in front of the stone.

"*Rest easy fair, Joan,*" she whispered. Before getting back to her feet and embracing Ian.

Caroline and Geoffrey also watched from the car. Seeing the tears in her eyes, he turned to Caroline, and said softly.

"*So it's over?*"

She smiled and laid her head on his shoulder.

"*Yes darling, I think it is.*"

FIN

Author's note

Queen Anne's curse is a work of fiction but is based on several true life events. The characters of Sir Michael Walker, Geoffrey Hawthorne, Caroline De Winter, Debbie and David Spencer, and Dr Ruth Walker, are based on real people; I have met during my career in both law enforcement and public life. The real Sir Michael Walker is a senior psychiatrist, from a Northern University in the UK, while the various Hampshire Constabulary officers are loosely based on colleagues who served with me in the last part of the 20th century.

Mystery still surrounds the sinking of the Mary Rose. Though most historians agree it was bad seamanship. However, there are still those who believe a more supernatural cause was responsible.

The recovery of the human remains from the ship enabled reconstructions of some of the crew using state-of-the-art computer generation and forensic facial recognition software. One of these was an Archer who was trapped below decks in a storehouse when the ship sank. This unknown sailor was the basis for the Mary Rose reconstruction, currently on display at the ship's museum in Portsmouth. Although there is limited information about this man, I have endeavoured to provide him with an identity based on a typical Tudor archer of the period who was on board the Mary Rose. His story is typical of those who served in Henry's navy in 1545. Many of the historic details of the history trail of the ring depicted in the book are real documented events, such as those surrounding Isadora Strauss and James Longstreet, and the fire that claimed the lives of some of Joan's descendants. As such, Queen Anne's Curse is a blend of fact and fiction where sometimes lines between them become blurred. This is not altogether unintentional.

Stephen C. Challis, February 2020

[]

www.ingramcontent.com/pod-product-compliance
Lightning Source LLC
Chambersburg PA
CBHW030319180626
46810CB00003B/1153